# THE **JOURNEY** PRIZE

TORIES

## WINNERS OF THE $10,000 JOURNEY PRIZE

1989
Holley Rubinsky for
"Rapid Transits"

1990
Cynthia Flood for "My Father
Took a Cake to France"

1991
Yann Martel for "The Facts
Behind the Helsinki Roccamatios"

1992
Rozena Maart for "No Rosa,
No District Six"

1993
Gayla Reid for
"Sister Doyle's Men"

1994
Melissa Hardy for
"Long Man the River"

1995
Kathryn Woodward for "Of
Marranos and Gilded Angels"

1996
Elyse Gasco for "Can You Wave
Bye Bye, Baby?"

1997 (shared)
Gabriella Goliger for
"Maladies of the Inner Ear"

Anne Simpson for
"Dreaming Snow"

1998
John Brooke for
"The Finer Points of Apples"

1999
Alissa York for "The Back of the
Bear's Mouth"

2000
Timothy Taylor for
"Doves of Townsend"

2001
Kevin Armstrong for
"The Cane Field"

2002
Jocelyn Brown for "Miss Canada"

2003
Jessica Grant for
"My Husband's Jump"

2004
Devin Krukoff for
"The Last Spark"

2005
Matt Shaw for "Matchbook for a
Mother's Hair"

2006
Heather Birrell for
"BriannaSusannaAlana"

2007
Craig Boyko for
"OZY"

# THE BEST OF CANADA'S NEW WRITERS
# THE **JOURNEY** PRIZE

### STORIES

SELECTED BY
LYNN **COADY**
HEATHER **O'NEILL**
NEIL **SMITH**

EMBLEM
McClelland & Stewart

A cataloguing record for this publication is available from Library and Archives Canada.

We acknowledge the financial support of the Government of Canada through the Book Publishing Industry Development Program and that of the Government of Ontario through the Ontario Media Development Corporation's Ontario Book Initiative. We further acknowledge the support of the Canada Council for the Arts and the Ontario Arts Council for our publishing program.

"At Last at Sea" © Sarah Steinberg; "Breaking on the Wheel" © Oscar Martens; "Chaperone" © Clea Young; "The Gifted Class" © Scott Randall; "Goodbye Porkpie Hat" © Mike Christie; "The Guiding Light" © Naomi K. Lewis; "My Three Girls" © Saleema Nawaz; "The Polar Bear at the Museum" © Anna Leventhal; "Some Light Down" © S. Kennedy Sobol; "Steaming for Godthab" © Dana Mills; "Whale Stories" © Théodora Armstrong.
These stories are reprinted with permission of the authors.

Typeset in Janson by M&S, Toronto
Printed and bound in Canada

ANCIENT FOREST
FRIENDLY

This book was produced using ancient-forest friendly papers.

McClelland & Stewart Ltd.
75 Sherbourne Street
Toronto, Ontario
M5A 2P9
www.mcclelland.com

1  2  3  4  5      12  11  10  09  08

The $10,000 Journey Prize is awarded annually to a new and developing writer of distinction. This award, now in its twentieth year, and given for the eighth time in association with the Writers' Trust of Canada as the Writers' Trust of Canada/McClelland & Stewart Journey Prize, is made possible by James A. Michener's generous donation of his Canadian royalty earnings from his novel *Journey*, published by McClelland & Stewart in 1988. The Journey Prize itself is the most significant monetary award given in Canada to a writer at the beginning of his or her career for a short story or excerpt from a fiction work in progress. The winner of this year's Journey Prize will be selected from among the eleven stories in this book.

*The Journey Prize Stories* has established itself as the most prestigious annual fiction anthology in the country, introducing readers to the finest new literary writers from coast to coast for two decades. It has become a who's who of up-and-coming writers, and many of the authors whose early work has appeared in the anthology's pages have gone on to distinguish themselves with collections of short stories, novels, and literary awards. The anthology comprises a selection from submissions made by the editors of literary journals from across the country, who have chosen what, in their view, is the most exciting writing in English that they have published in the previous year. In recognition of the vital role journals play in discovering new writers, McClelland & Stewart makes its own award of $2,000 to the journal that originally published and submitted the winning entry.

This year the selection jury, comprising multi-award-winning writers Lynn Coady, Heather O'Neill, and Neil Smith, read a total of seventy-five submissions without knowing the names of the authors or those of the journals in which the stories had originally appeared. McClelland & Stewart would like to thank the jury for their efforts in selecting this year's anthology and, ultimately, the winner of this year's Journey Prize.

McClelland & Stewart would also like to acknowledge the continuing enthusiastic support of writers, literary journal editors, and the public in the common celebration of the emergence of new voices in Canadian fiction.

For more information about *The Journey Prize Stories*, please consult our website: www.mcclelland.com/jps.

# CONTENTS

*Congratulations to the Journey Prize – from the Authors*  ix

*Reading the 2008 Journey Prize Stories*  xix
Lynn Coady, Heather O'Neill, Neil Smith

## CLEA YOUNG
Chaperone  1
(from *Grain Magazine*)

## OSCAR MARTENS
Breaking on the Wheel  19
(from *Queen's Quarterly*)

## NAOMI K. LEWIS
The Guiding Light  29
(from *The Fiddlehead*)

## DANA MILLS
Steaming for Godthab  62
(from *Geist*)

## THÉODORA ARMSTRONG
Whale Stories  75
(from *Event*)

## MIKE CHRISTIE
Goodbye Porkpie Hat  93
(from *subTerrain Magazine*)

**SCOTT RANDALL**
The Gifted Class 120
(from *The Dalhousie Review*)

**S. KENNEDY SOBOL**
Some Light Down 135
(from *PRISM international*)

**SARAH STEINBERG**
At Last at Sea 163
(from *This Magazine*)

**ANNA LEVENTHAL**
The Polar Bear at the Museum 171
(from *Geist*)

**SALEEMA NAWAZ**
My Three Girls 180
(from *Prairie Fire*)

*About the Authors* 193
*About the Contributing Journals* 196
*Previous Contributing Authors* 202

## CAROLINE ADDERSON

"I was naturally thrilled to have a story included in the *Journey Prize* anthology. Particularly when you're just starting out, being accepted in an anthology – an actual book instead of a magazine, something with a spine, something that people might buy in a bookstore – feels like donning a tiara. But it wasn't until I sat on the Journey Prize jury myself fourteen years later that I realized how tough the competition is, how many stories are submitted, and how many good ones aren't included for lack of space or jury consensus. If I'd known this back then, I probably wouldn't have settled for that tiara feeling. I'd have gone around with the darned book strapped to my head."

## ANDRÉ ALEXIS

"Being nominated for the Journey Prize made me feel as if my choice to be a writer was not entirely wayward. Of course, I had friends who encouraged me, friends who also wrote (better than I did, some of them), but . . . there is nothing like the approval of strangers to make you feel you're on the right track. Not that the nomination was more important than the opinion of my friends, the (obsessive) reading I did, the music I listened to, the sheer, ceaseless thinking about writing, but . . .

it simply made me feel I had (at least once) managed to make my private universe available to those with no vested interest in me whatsoever. That – a kind of recognition across a divide – gave me a confidence in the road I had chosen. I might still be mistaken for devoting my life to writing. There is still time for all to end badly, but . . . if there is some ledger, some means of tabulating the positive (on one side) and the negative (on the other), the Journey Prize nomination is (almost certainly) on the good side of things. . . . In any case, I am still writing, and I am grateful to James Michener, to McClelland & Stewart, to the jury that gave me a (sadly brief) confidence in my work."

## DAVID BERGEN

"Way back in 1989, I got lucky with my first published story when it was selected for the *Journey Prize* anthology. Then I got lucky three more times. It is astounding to see how many writers published in the anthology over the last twenty years have gone on to publish great story collections and novels. The anthology is a windfall for both writer and reader."

## DENNIS BOCK

"A great jolt of electricity startles the heart and jump-starts the writing career when you get the nod from the Journey people. It's a thrill to find your name included amongst some of the leading new voices in short fiction."

## CRAIG DAVIDSON

"I was distressed to find out that not everyone who is included in the *Journey Prize* anthology can expect to publish a much-loved worldwide bestseller and win the Booker Prize, as Yann Martel did, after he somehow eked into the anthology years before my own appearance (oh, right, and won). Setting that unhappy realization aside, being a part of the anthology was something of a landmark in my own progression as a writer. I'd read previous editions, and to be a part of it myself was a great surprise. It provided me with some confidence, a commodity highly prized by writers, especially when you're just starting out. Now, if you'll excuse me, I have to go walk Yann Martel's dog for him."

## ELYSE FRIEDMAN

"I was thrilled to have a piece included in *The Journey Prize Stories*. It's one of the best showcases for short fiction in Canada."

## JESSICA GRANT

"Many years ago, a kind relative who knew I had literary aspirations gave me a copy of the *Journey Prize* anthology. It was bright red and contained stories by new Canadian writers. Would I ever be one of those? So far I was just Canadian. A decade later I got a phone call that changed my life. Are you sitting down? I was living in a tiny apartment in Calgary and I had one chair. I was so excited I couldn't find my one chair. Wait, wait! I sat down on the floor.

I had won the Journey Prize! How did I feel? Like a super-hero. Very proud. Very grateful. And completely cured of my worst fear – that I wouldn't be a writer."

## TERRY GRIGGS

"The name is felicitous, the company excellent, the honour ongoing. To have a story selected for the *Journey Prize* anthology at the beginning of one's publishing life is like being given a lucky charm for the uncertain journey ahead. It opens doors (and eyes), provides encouragement and solace when needed, and offers assurance that there are indeed those who value the effort and artistry involved. This marvellous annual collection heralds and celebrates exciting new talent, and lets that talent know a steadily growing audience is waiting, and listening."

## ELIZABETH HAY

"What a thrill! A yes instead of a no. I had done something right, and now I would have to figure out what it was."

## STEVEN HEIGHTON

"I remember feeling ratified, authenticated, which of course was an illusion; no journal or anthology or prize ever proves you a real writer (whatever that is). But being chosen for an important anthology like the *Journey Prize* gave me a lift when I especially needed one, and I think of that with gratitude, admiration."

## FRANCES ITANI

"The writing apprenticeship is a long one, perhaps never-ending, and an appearance in the *Journey Prize* anthology is a boost of encouragement along the way. I am especially pleased that several of my former students have been included. Bravo for continuing to celebrate this challenging and exact genre – the story in its short form."

## MARK ANTHONY JARMAN

"The telegram, the telephone call, the electric jolt of a shot at $10,000 for a story and a banner unfurling in your brain. What are the odds? Very good odds, an antidote to discouraging words, to be acknowledged, a visitation in the boondock wilderness – no one knows you – hidden deep in the gymnasium's wallflower shadows and asked to dance. You step forward. The telegram, the telephone ringing, an electric jolt, and you float over the provinces, tickled pink as your map of Canada."

## ELISE LEVINE

"Being in the *Journey Prize* anthology – alongside all those other cakewalking babies – emboldened me enough to feel I could keep pursuing the kind of stories I really wanted to tell. Each year's anthology is like a kind of boulevard of promise, with the bright lights of so many fully developed, book-length works to come – by interesting, gifted writers – winking just up the road."

## PASHA MALLA

"David Bergen is a loser. André Alexis: also a loser. Anne Carson, Lee Henderson, Heather O'Neill – all losers. And I can claim to losing the Journey Prize not once, but *twice* myself.

I guess it should be reassuring to be in the company of some of Canada's best and brightest. The honourable thing would be to celebrate even being included in *The Journey Prize Stories*, offer kudos to the two talented writers (Matt Shaw in 2006 and Craig Boyko last year) who have beaten me for Canada's richest short story prize, and go about my way.

But, see, I'm not much for sportsmanship. Jealousy and resentment are more my thing. Also, coincidentally enough, the balance owing on my student loan is right around $10,000.

Being in the company of all these beautiful losers is fine and good, but ten grand for twenty pages of typing? I don't harbour any particular ill will toward Shaw and Boyko, but, literary accolades aside, it would have been *awesome* to win."

## YANN MARTEL

"In a matter of a few years, the *Journey Prize* anthology has become the proving ground for new, young Canadian writers, a who's who of the coming generation. You've been published in this and that literary review, great – but have you been published in the *Journey Prize* anthology? For many young writers (myself included), it's their first appearance in a 'real' book by a 'real' publisher. After that, letters from editors get a lot more polite, even if they're rejections. The *Journey Prize* anthology is important to young writers because it is unique. There's nothing else like it in Canada. Writers who are 'big,' 'established,' 'older,' 'mature' – whatever you want to call them – have a panoply of prizes to honour them. . . . But for young writers, it's the Journey Prize or nothing. . . . I, for one, owe everything to the Journey Prize; I don't mean the money – I mean the attention, the publicity, the boost in confidence. . . . For obvious reasons, I remember the Journey Prize with fondness. It got the ball rolling for me."

## EDEN ROBINSON

"I remember buying twenty copies of the fourth *Journey Prize* anthology, and giving them out to family for Christmas with my story helpfully Post-it marked. I finally got up the courage to ask a cousin what he thought of it, and he said, 'Yeah. It was long. Didn't finish it.' Which seemed to be the reaction of most of my family, except for my mom and dad, who kept their copy on the coffee table. The press and the attention I received from being in the anthology were important to my career, but not as crucial as my family finally referring to me as The Writer instead of The Most Educated Bum in Kitamaat Village."

## ANNE SIMPSON

"When the Journey Prize was established in 1989, I recall reading a *Globe and Mail* article about the first winner, Holley Rubinsky. I never thought I'd have a short story included in the *Journey Prize* anthology eight years later. The door that opened for me in 1997 – one I imagined was a huge, locked door that might have been custom-made for the gods in Valhalla – stayed open. And I'm still a bit amazed that the door opened and that it has remained open since then."

## NEIL SMITH

"I owe a huge debt to the Journey Prize. Before my nominations, I didn't even know I wanted to be a writer. I saw my writing as arts and crafts, nothing more serious than macaroni that's spray-painted gold and glued to a tissue box.

When my first story got nominated, I thought, Fluke. When a second story got the nod, I thought, Another fluke. When a third story was picked, I thought, Career change!

If there were no Journey Prize, I wouldn't have kept writing. I wouldn't be sitting in a room all alone, making up stuff in my head. Obsessing over my fiction. Looking at somebody and thinking what a great character he'd make in my novel.

When people ask how I've changed since publishing my first book, I reply that I'm now more neurotic but also more content. So big thanks to the Journey Prize and McClelland & Stewart for feeding my neurosis and making me a happier person."

## TIMOTHY TAYLOR

"Quite a few years before I would have dared call myself a writer in public, while I was still working at a bank, I began to buy the *Journey Prize* anthology yearly. I did so because I understood it to collect the best new short fiction of the year, and I hoped quietly that I would be inspired. One afternoon, a colleague caught me reading the anthology at my desk. Knowing a little about my literary interests, he asked bluntly: Are you in it this year? I wasn't, and I said so. But after he left my office, I remember my astonishment, my disbelief at his suggestion. These are 'real' writers (I wanted to shout), and while I aspire in the same direction, I have yet to publish a single story! About eight years later, I was included in the anthology and I remembered my colleague. It occurred to me that – despite the years I'd been at it and the stories that had since been published – nothing up to that point had convinced me that I could be a real writer. And while I remained astonished to see my name in those pages, the *Journey Prize* anthology now marked a beginning in which I could really believe. I've continued to read the anthology, and count it as an honour to have adjudicated during its fifteenth year. To me, its ongoing contribution is found on every page: new writers, new voices, new confidence."

## MADELEINE THIEN

"'Simple Recipes' was my first published story, and the one that, to my utter amazement, made it into the *Journey Prize* anthology. I remember getting the phone call, and remember sitting on the couch for a long time staring at the wall. I had a strange sense of vertigo, to think that it might actually be possible to one day write a book, and for that book one day to find readers. I had always quietly hoped for that possibility, but hadn't really thought it was within the boundaries of reality until that day."

## ALISSA YORK

"After a decade of writing fiction, I find to my amazement that the greatest imaginative feat required of me thus far has been the conception of myself as a writer. Every published story helped, but the day I learned my work was to be included in the eleventh volume of the *Journey Prize* anthology – and thereby in a national tradition of literary discovery – was the day when the writer I had long been imagining finally began to seem real."

## LYNN COADY

What is it about short fiction anyway? It's loved and lamented, ignored and eulogized. We're told short fiction collections "don't sell" and that "no one" reads them, and yet countless elephantine story anthologies are shipped yearly to universities, and the most respected practitioners of the form, people like Alice Munro and Lorrie Moore, are discussed with the kind of superstitious awe you'd expect might be reserved for shamans and priests in days gone by. A great novelist is honoured, but – with a few exceptions – still manages to seem of this earth. A truly great short story writer, however, is near-revered. This doesn't strike me as being completely out of line, somehow.

I've always found short fiction to be the more uncanny of the prose forms, and I think the reason for this lies in Elizabeth Bowen's concept of "poetic truth," which she claims is the ultimate aim of all prose writing, whether long or short. Short fiction seems to lend itself more readily to this concept than the novel. As a genre, it has always seemed to me just a little more poetic, more literary – freer to play the holy fool, to explore the mysterious and the strange, the ambivalent and random. In novels, qualities like ambivalence and randomness don't go over as well. A short story, simply by virtue of its shortness, is indulged by the reader the same way a younger child is indulged by a parent. Let's extend the metaphor and think of the novel as the older sibling: she might get more attention and respect, but should she give voice to a dreamy disposition, she will impatiently be told to "talk sense" after a while. The younger child, meanwhile, is permitted to free-associate and babble, to splash around in his own subconscious.

It's the difference, I think, between the stuff you need to build a church and the stuff you need to pray in one: one requires a great deal of skill, the other a great deal of vision, but each endeavour requires the other in a fundamental way. The difference between the novel and the short story, then, is one of balance – work in balance with play, craft with art. Plot, for example – that mundane, plodding demand of causality and coherence – is work. Any novelist will tell you so. The reason so many novelists will stop in the middle of arduous revisions to bang off a short story is because they want to get back to the "play" of writing. I can't recall ever having deliberately plotted a piece of short fiction the way I have a novel. And I've certainly never finished writing a novel by simply stopping – looking down at the page and realizing with a jolt, "I'm finished!" – which is how most of my short fiction has wrapped itself up. That's the quality that makes short fiction just a little more magical as far as I'm concerned. I'd bet cash money it's the quality that gets most new writers hooked.

Of course, to write a good short story, one that comes across as satisfying and inevitable and true, still requires a sharp set of craftsman's tools. The stories chosen for this year's *Journey Prize Stories* are exemplars of art and craft in perfect balance. They are the work of authors who are skilled enough to have mastered their tools, but also gifted with a distinct creative vision.

Everything about "The Guiding Light," sitting quietly among the riotous cluster of stories that vied in various colourful ways for the jury's attention, seems counterintuitive. First there is its sedate title, smacking of soap operas and just a whiff of the New Age. Then there is its straightforward perspective, its total eschewal of "quirk" in voice and subject matter. Here is a story not just about grown-ups, but, by God, the middle-aged – middle-aged *women*. It's a story about people weighed down (or emphatically not, in the case of Virginia Morgan) with the quotidian obligations of families, cars, and dogs, with financial and career apprehensions, yet a story that manages to achieve, amidst such middle-class banality, a stealthy, inexorable sense of the strange – of deepening unease and, yes, mystery. The story is further unfashionable in its length, its understated language, and its lack of structural pyrotechnics. Innovation done well and with confidence can be a tonic to the jaded literary jurist, but more often than not, a quiet piece of writing that takes its own sweet time to unfold and is crafted to perfection can be every bit as thrilling. It's like immersing yourself in a warm, placid lake only to be blindsided, after your first few strokes, by how exhilarating it is.

Oscar Marten's "Breaking on the Wheel," however, is more like when a sadistic friend, already wet, takes it upon herself to direct a few invigorating splashes your way. There are moments in this story that hit you with a similarly innerving impact – innerving and unnerving – as when Dana brings a little boy to tears with her laboriously manufactured smile, or the instant she realizes her "horrible power" to achieve precisely the opposite effect on customers from what her father believes a "happy" little girl should have. Dana's obsession with the concepts of "fun" and "happiness" are utterly and tragically academic, and this realization is a shock that stays with a reader for days.

"Steaming for Godthab"'s particular strangeness is the strangeness of the visceral present – when the past and the future and all outside context fall away, leaving a group of sailors with nothing but their most immediate experiences of loathing and desire and disgust in one another's seemingly eternal presence. Dana Mills's accomplishment here is in the desperate velocity of his narrator's first-person, present-tense voice. Mills grabs you by the throat from the story's very beginning and aims, as it were, a narrative fork at your eye. Which is to say, he gets your attention and keeps it.

Sarah Steinberg's "At Last at Sea" picks up on that same vertiginous shipboard weirdness – the queasy moment you find yourself without context, "at sea" both literally and figuratively: "No newspapers, no cooking, no cash, and the only thing to see out the window is ocean." Steinberg's genius lies in her rendering of subtext, in all the story doesn't say, alongside moments so vivid yet so quick and offhand you might easily make the mistake of supposing Steinberg isn't placing every word with the precision of a miniaturist painter. The mother's "deep, miserable laugh" that punctuates mealtime small talk is a detail only a resentful, guilt-ridden daughter could pick up on, and is consequently gut-wrenching.

I should clarify that in my personal critical lexicon *gut-wrenching* is one of the highest compliments an author can receive. All the stories in this year's *Journey Prize* anthology wrenched the jury's guts in one way or another, meaning they had a visceral effect – the stories reached inside us and shuffled things around. Their authors are to be congratulated for their insight, fearlessness, and skill. The literary journals that first published them are to be congratulated for their discernment – not to mention the simple fact of allowing Canadian short fiction to thrive in their pages. They deserve our thanks for their continued indulgence and encouragement of literature's unruly, visionary younger sibling.

LYNN COADY was nominated for the 1998 Governor General's Literary Award for Fiction for her first novel, *Strange Heaven*. She received the Canadian Authors Association/Air Canada Award for the best writer under thirty and the Dartmouth Book and Writing Award for fiction. Her second book, *Play the Monster Blind*, was a national bestseller and a *Globe and Mail* "Best Book" of 2000; *Saints of Big Harbour*, also a bestseller, was a *Globe and Mail* "Best Book" in 2002. Her latest novel, *Mean Boy*, was a *Globe and Mail* "Best Book" of 2006 and the winner of the Writers Guild of Alberta's George Bugnet Award for Fiction. Most recently, she acted as editor on *The Anansi Reader: 40 Years of Very Good Books*. Lynn Coady lives in Toronto.

## HEATHER O'NEILL

Becoming a writer can feel a little bit like being Dr. Frankenstein. You labour away at it, creating monsters for years: they live and breathe, but they are imperfect, and you end up despising them. Just the same, even though you've written things that make no sense, bore your friends to tears, and get rejected by all the magazines, you refuse to give up. Then one day you discover that you have created something small, maybe even just a paragraph, and that little thing is beautiful. It won't come back to haunt you, but it makes you proud. The stories in this anthology reflect the excitement of that moment.

"Goodbye Porkpie Hat" is a wonderfully erudite and gritty story. I absolutely loved this story. I thought it was a brilliant spin on the genre of junkie narratives. The language and attention to detail are wonderful and pitch perfect. It is cool, edgy, and intellectual. The narrator is at once brilliantly observant and wildly amoral. I found this story stood out for me because of the sophistication and maturity of its writing. It also vividly opened up a whole world for me within the very first sentences. It is reminiscent of the best of William Burroughs and reveals a great talent.

"The Polar Bear at the Museum" is a whimsical tour de force that describes the ugliness of being a teenage girl while somehow also revealing the beauty. It recreates the period of late childhood in a breathless, utterly raw way. It is evocative of the way teenagers think – of the pettiness of their concerns and the magnitude of their capacity for observation and grace. It is totally entertaining and joyous.

"Some Light Down" captures the way in which children react to the abduction of other children their own age. It also mirrors, through a clever pastiche of voices, the way in which we assemble knowledge in order to feel and understand tragedy collectively. This piece was included in this anthology because of the breadth of the tale that it manages to tell and the skill it employs in doing so. It is heartbreaking and wise.

I really enjoyed all the stories in this anthology. I find the effect of reading them to be like listening to a great late-night DJ who has gone out of his way to find brand new, totally exciting, up-and-coming bands.

HEATHER O'NEILL is the author of *Lullabies for Little Criminals*, which won the 2007 edition of CBC's Canada Reads and the Hugh MacLennan Prize for Fiction, and was a finalist for the Orange Prize, the Governor General's Award, the Amazon.ca/ Books in Canada First Novel Award, and the Grand Prix du Livre de Montreal. A two-time nominee for the Journey Prize, O'Neill is a contributor to *This American Life* and *Wiretap*, and her work has appeared in the *New York Times Magazine*. She lives in Montreal.

## NEIL SMITH

*The Burned Children of Canada*. I have always wanted to edit an anthology of stories and call it that. I've stolen the title from my all-time favourite American anthology, *The Burned Children of America*. The book features wave-making, risk-taking stories by youngish writers like George Saunders, Judy Budnitz, A.M. Homes, Aimee Bender, Matthew Klam, and Jonathan Safran Foer. In her intro to the book, Zadie Smith wonders why these American writers are so burned, why "one smells a certain sadness coming off them" even when they're being funny.

Well, we Canadians can be melancholy too. We can be sad and droll at the same time. We can be creepy. We can be burned. Hence, *The Burned Children of Canada*. Think of the young writers you'd want in such a book. I bet most have graced the pages of *The Journey Prize Stories* over the years, including daring writers like Craig Davidson, Pasha Malla, Charlotte Gill, Annabel Lyon, Craig Boyko, Elyse Friedman, and Heather O'Neill.

As I waded through submissions for the latest *Journey Prize* anthology, sad, burned children mustn't have been far from my mind given the stories my fellow jurors and I picked.

In Théodora Armstrong's "Whale Stories," young William ensnares a wild dog in a deep hole he's dug and set with bait. The injured mutt whimpers and yelps, and William is torn. He had thought he was doing "real man's work" by building his trap, but now he reveals himself to be a troubled little boy who, panic-stricken, commits a cruel, irrevocable act. This haunting story is about the holes we dig ourselves into and the lies we tell to cover them up.

A whole cast of Gashlycrumb Tinies pops up in Scott Randall's "The Gifted Class." These polite second-graders matter-of-factly discuss the merits of Dexedrine versus Ritalin, common-law relationships versus marriage, and chicken noodle soup versus tomato. No characters in the submissions I read made me laugh as much as little Belman, Marla, and Billy. They speak like Linus from *Peanuts*. But again, there's that sadness. I practically got a lump in my throat when Belman, anxious about a class presentation, earnestly confides to Marla, "I get nervous sometimes." To borrow a favourite word from the children's teacher, "The Gifted Class" is grand.

An embalmed baby girl with a mottled blue and red face hovers like an evil spirit over Saleema Nawaz's story "My Three Girls." The dead baby seems to be watching her sisters and parents, and striking them down if they show "signs of too much happiness." This tightly written piece accomplishes the impressive feat of condensing a novel's worth of sorrows and joys into a few pages.

In Clea Young's "Chaperone," a doormat of a dad accompanies young students on a field trip to a hot springs resort. After a showdown with his defiant fourteen-year-old daughter, the father realizes that to keep his family together, he must be more than merely a chaperone in the girl's life. Clea Young nails the snarkiness of teens testing their independence and the weariness of a father baffled by his responsibilities. But what makes the story really shine is its empathy and honesty.

Is there sadness emanating from these four writers? You bet. Have Théodora, Scott, Saleema, Clea, and the other writers in this anthology become part of my stable of burned children of Canada? They have. More importantly, though, they've become Journey Prize authors. So let me fire up the branding iron and burn a little JP into their shoulders (beside their inoculation scars). In the coming years, they'll find that this mark of distinction will open doors and put them in very good company.

I for one wear that JP on my shoulder as if it were a big fancy gold epaulette. *Un gros merci* to McClelland & Stewart and editor Anita Chong for igniting my writing career and the careers of so many other burned children of Canada.

NEIL SMITH is the author of *Bang Crunch*, a book of stories that is being published internationally. Three stories included in the collection were nominated for the Journey Prize. The book itself won the McAuslan First Book Prize, was shortlisted for the Commonwealth Writers' Prize for Best First Book and the Hugh MacLennan Prize, and was chosen as a "Best Book" of 2007 by the *Globe and Mail* and *Le Devoir*. His next book is a novel about the afterlife called *Heaven Is a Place Where Nothing Ever Happens*. For more details, visit his website: www.bangcrunch.com.

# THE **JOURNEY** PRIZE

STORIES

# CLEA YOUNG

## CHAPERONE

**H**olt turned twice beneath a shower nozzle before exiting the change room through a heavy cedar door. Outside, snowflakes fizzled on his skin. To his right, he saw his daughter, Beth, neck-deep in a hot tub, surrounded by class-mates. A few feet from the hot tub was a smaller, waterfall-fed pool with a sign that read: POLAR BEAR PLUNGE! Beneath the slapping water, a dark, muscular man wrung and rewrung a whip of long black hair.

"Ugh," Beth grunted in Holt's direction. "You look naked," she said.

"Just about," Holt said.

"Your shorts," she said.

Holt looked down at his legs.

"They're *beige*. Like your skin."

Holt struck a pose, one hand on his hip, the other behind his head, a pin-up girl. He could see the kids assessing the pouchy flesh above his knees. The bristled wings of hair on his shoulders. The brutal scar where he'd had his appendix removed as a child.

"Spare us," Beth said. She turned from Holt and waved as if to shoo him away. Holt returned her gesture, grossly exaggerated, as a younger brother might, but Beth didn't see. She lunged through the frothy water and into the steaming mouth of a cave, the origin of the hot springs. Holt watched her head bob into the darkness, and, shortly, those of the other children who fell into formation behind her.

Holt rose onto his toes to distance himself from the stinging concrete. He eyed the Hercules of a man, still preening beneath the icy waterfall. The man's abdomen was girded with muscle and swashbuckling hoops hung from his nipples. Holt flinched at the thought of a needle piercing the epicentre of so many nerve endings. He hugged his own flabby girth and let out an involuntary yip at the effect of the cold. Then he waded into the larger pool, a not-hot-enough bath, pressing air from his shorts' pockets. In the deep end, Beth's social studies teacher, Wanda, and another chaperone, an athletic dad named Barry, were seated on a submerged ledge. As he crouched through the water toward them, Holt surveyed the resort's impressive view of Stamina Lake. From this height, halfway up a mountain, the lake's ice-chunked surface appeared so still, so compliant with the confines of its banks, that Holt had the impression he was looking down on a diorama.

"They behaving in there?" Barry asked when Holt was within earshot. He widened his eyes in the direction of the cave.

"God knows what they're doing," Wanda said. "I don't even *want* to know. I started teaching when I was twenty-four, and every year they come with a new bag of tricks."

"Hold up," Barry said. "Twenty-four? You started teaching last year?"

"Ha-ha," Wanda said. She flicked watery fingers in Barry's face. "*You* might not think so," she said, "but the kids think I'm prehistoric."

Wanda had a big mouth, lips that seemed to slide all over her face when she spoke. She was captivating and grotesque. Holt drifted onto the ledge, next to her, leaving a calculated space between their bodies.

"We were just talking about magnet-head," Barry said.

"Right," said Holt. "The girl."

"They'll have to be punished," said Wanda, wearily. Then she turned to Holt and said, "Barry's already suggested cancelling the rest of these field trips, but *I* like this. I don't know about you guys, but I'd be marking if I was at home."

"I wasn't thinking," Barry apologized. "Everyone needs to get away. Just forget what I said."

A sizzle of red on the inside of Barry's right bicep snagged Holt's gaze.

"That a tattoo?" he said.

"Yeah," said Barry. He lifted his arm from the water and flexed his muscle. A loonie-sized maple leaf tightened across his skin. "Product of Canada, baby," he said.

"Gentlemen, please," Wanda said.

"All right," said Holt. "So, what do you propose?"

"Well –" Wanda tilted her head back against the concrete lip of the pool and pinched her eyes. A heat-fattened arterial vein ran the length of her neck. Holt watched it throb fitfully, in time with her heart. He and Barry waited for the woman to speak, for her mutant lips to produce a judgment. This waiting. Holt felt as if he were in conference with his wife, Claudette, about Beth. Should they ground her or just shorten her curfew? No television? Take away her cellphone? Holt was tired of discipline. Nothing worked.

"You're a doormat," Claudette had said when, after rehashing the same problems for months, he'd quit offering solutions and, quite literally, lay down on their bedroom floor. Claudette ground her socked heel between his shoulder blades.

"She just walks all over you," his wife growled, toes plucking at his back muscles, not unlike a massage.

"The dust bunnies down here," Holt groaned.

"So, get a goddamn broom." Claudette spurred him in the ribs and left the room.

Holt remained with his ear to the floor, listening to his wife's footsteps punch down the stairs and into the kitchen below. The suction of the fridge door opening. The thwap of a few bags of produce landing on the countertop. A dull knife drawn from the drawer.

"We all know detentions don't work," Wanda said, opening her eyes. "And besides, that wouldn't be fair because I'm fairly certain *some* kids are more to blame." She looked conspiratorially to Barry. Holt sensed where they were going.

"Your daughter's a leader," Wanda said.

"Beth," said Holt.

"She's got charisma," Barry said. "You know?" He cupped his hands and tossed water over one shoulder, then the other, a gesture, Holt thought, that recalled some sort of ancient bathing ritual performed by old men in the Ganges.

"She *is* outgoing," Holt said.

Wanda snorted, "She's certainly not shy."

"Hey," said Holt. He didn't like her tone.

Wanda lifted herself from the pool to sit on the edge. "It's hot in there," she panted. She gave Barry's shoulder a cautionary pat. "You don't realize how hot."

"Look, Holt," said Barry. "We think Beth had something to do with last night."

"Sure. Maybe," said Holt. "But she couldn't have been the only one."

"I wouldn't call her manipulative –" Wanda said. She shivered audibly, then laughed. "Phew," she said, "this is cold on my bum." She stood on the submerged ledge, between the two men.

Holt drifted a little; Wanda's thigh was suddenly too close to his face.

"You're serious about this," he said.

Barry shrugged.

Wanda reached up and adjusted the bathing-suit strings behind her neck. Her newly shaved underarms, raw and puckered like chicken flesh, at once disgusted Holt and struck him as utterly vain. "Because it's quite the accusation to make," he continued, shooting them a look he hoped conveyed both warning and disdain. Wanda squinted at him but said nothing. He could tell she thought he was being hyperdefensive, and her coolness, her critical stare, made him wonder if he wasn't acting irrationally. He should have just laughed it off, but it was too late now. Holt tipped his head back into the water and ran his hands through his hair. A murder of crows was flying overhead. Wanda was right, the pool was hotter than he'd first realized.

———

Last night it had been Holt's turn to enforce the curfew. He hadn't wanted to. At eleven o'clock he'd already been in bed for an hour, pleasantly sedated – the heat in his room cranked, back-to-back reruns of *Cheers*. For a minute or two, before mobilizing, he lay staring up at the jagged stucco ceiling and imagined neglecting his duty. What if he just fell asleep? He closed his eyes and indulged his weariness. At this hour, who could blame him? But if something happened to any one of the kids, he knew Wanda would blame him. The other parents would blame him. And of course, he would blame himself.

Holt pulled the too small courtesy bathrobe from its hanger in the closet and shoved his bare feet into a pair of snow-soggy shoes. Outside his room, the hotel halls were chilly and dimly lit; each corridor looked the same. On the elevator landing, he paused and tried to remember the way to the kids' rooms. A side table and two wingback chairs were arranged there, as if it was some place a person might like to sit, and Holt sat in one of the chairs. On the table, with a few slick travel magazines, there was a potted orchid, its single stem held upright with what looked like skewers. He touched the white petals and wasn't too surprised to find them fake. An elevator arrived and dinged open to reveal no one. Holt wasn't sure if he should be riding the carriage up or down so he didn't move. The doors slid shut and his reflection appeared before him. In the bleary metal, he saw a man holding his robe closed at the throat in a manner that resembled a modest housewife who'd opened her front door to an unannounced visitor, wary, but curious at the same time. He also saw that his legs were crossed, a position Beth often snarked was too feminine for a man. Still, he didn't move.

On the wall above him, a sepia photograph showed the hot springs as they had looked in the 1920s, before ski lifts had been strung up the mountainside, before the resort had been built. Because he couldn't bring himself to stand, to sacrifice the warm patch he'd created on the chair, he strained to read the caption beneath the photo. At the time the picture was taken, a mining company had owned the land and had excavated the area's first crude swimming pool for the benefit of its employees. But for hundreds of years before that, the land had been a summer camp – and no doubt a place of spiritual significance – for the Natives during their annual huckleberry harvest. Holt liked to think of the place as it had been before the cement was poured and the pool floor painted aquamarine. He liked to imagine a tribe stripping off their garb, their baskets and buckskins, and easing into the natural pools. He also liked to imagine the miners inviting their wives or girlfriends up for an innocent swim, those demure women who, in the photograph, wore bathing caps and swimsuits that covered their thighs.

Holt shivered. The cold had distracted him. He'd forgotten why he was there, on the elevator landing, fingering a fake orchid's petals. He decided that some employee must have mistaken air conditioning for heat, and so far no one had complained. He would go to the front desk and inquire.

It was then, as he thought of how to phrase his complaint to the hotel clerk, that he heard muffled laughter and some sort of rhythmic beat, chanting maybe. Had it just begun, or was he only tuning in to it now? Holt rose from the chair and scuffed in the direction of the sound, past an ice machine producing small internal avalanches, past the open door to a supplies room displaying stacked linens and spray bottles of blue liquid. He felt as though he were navigating a medieval castle; the wall lighting was torchlike, flickering. The chanting, sacrificial. It amplified as he approached the end of the hall.

He heard more clearly: "Mag-net-head, mag-net-head, mag-net-head." He was standing outside the room Beth shared with three girls.

Holt put his ear to the door. Inside, he heard the congested voices of boys in the throes of puberty, the idiotic twittering of girls who weren't dumb. He heard his heart chugging out of its earlier stupor. Naturally, the door was locked.

"Hey," Holt said. "Open up." He rattled the handle before remembering that his room key, one of those credit-card types, had been programmed to access all of the kids' rooms. He pulled the card from his robe pocket and slid it into the lock.

What hit him first was the smell. A roomful of kids who didn't yet practise the daily swipe of underarm deodorant, who didn't yet realize the smell was coming from them. He'd taken only one or two strides toward the balcony doors, which he intended to open, when he saw the girl. She was passed out on the floor between the two beds, haloed with crushed beer cans, welts ripening on her forehead. He stopped to better assess the situation. He scanned the room. Boys and girls were sprawled across the floor and beds, limbs overlapping. Like a bunch of five-year-olds, pretending to be asleep. Some convulsed with restrained laughter. Holt tried to single out Beth in the dog pile. He looked for a hand or a foot.

---

A flake caught on Holt's eyelashes and blurred his vision. He lifted his head from the water and said, "Your son's no pushover." Barry's kid was a waifish, loud-mouthed boy.

"Whoa," Barry said. "Careful now."

Wanda had slipped back into the pool. She stood a few feet before the men with her hands on her hips.

"This isn't the Spanish Inquisition," she said. She raised one foot from the water and wiggled her toes. "Hey you!" she yelped when Barry grabbed her ankle. "Can't you see I'm doing a leg regime?" She floundered unconvincingly.

Barry maintained his grip on Wanda's ankle. He said to Holt, "This is about magnet-head and your daughter. *Some*body had to get that beer."

"Need I remind you," said Holt, pausing as a great surge of blood rushed to his head, "that Beth is four*teen*?"

"She has a way with men," Wanda said, "that, as a father, I think you choose not to see."

"With *men*," said Holt, incredulous, panting. His balance faltered; had he not been supported by water, he would have staggered, but neither Barry nor Wanda noticed.

"She's tall," Wanda went on. "She puts herself together – let's just say, she's more womanly than other girls her age."

What the hell was she talking about? Beth was coltish and breastless. As far as Holt could see, there wasn't anything *womanly* about her except that, sometimes, he glimpsed bits of Claudette in Beth – her small mouth that revealed very few teeth when she smiled – but that was it; the extent to which Beth was a woman was apparent only in the way she would one day come to look like her mother.

"They got a bootlegger," Barry said. "Beth must have convinced some guy."

Some guy, indeed. The resort village had only one liquor store and it was located directly across the street from the hotel. Holt had picked up a case of beer so that he might have a few when he returned to his room after a weary day spent tracking kids on the ski hill. He'd nestled the bottles in a snowdrift on his balcony and was pleased that they'd chilled thoroughly but hadn't frozen.

"Since your daughter doesn't live with you and Claudia –" Wanda said.

"Claudette," Holt said.

"Right," said Wanda. "Isn't it possible you're a little out of touch?"

Holt didn't think so, nor did he think theirs a particularly unusual situation. Beth was taking a break from him and Claudette, living with his older sister, Marcia, a ten-minute drive from their home. Marcia had already been through this kind of thing. Her eldest daughter, now at university, had dropped out of school at fifteen to follow her boyfriend to an ashram, then down to Baja in a Winnebago. When she fell out of the boyfriend's favour, she hitched all the way home.

"It's fine," Marcia had assured Holt when he phoned to make the arrangements.

"It won't be for long," he promised.

"She's a good kid," Marcia said. "Really, it's fine."

And apparently she was good to Marcia, said please and thank you and emptied the dishwasher without being told.

In his periphery, Holt saw that the crows were still flying overhead. Maybe they weren't flying at all; they appeared to be suspended by fishing line, part of the diorama he felt he was in. The mountain on the opposite side of Stamina Lake, which had earlier been obscured by low cloud, now loomed impossibly near. Holt felt he could distinguish each tree from the next, each one's unique hood of snow.

"It could be your name," Holt said, finally.

"Excuse me?" Wanda said.

"Why the kids think you're old. Wanda. It's from another generation."

Wanda flushed her arms through the water. She appeared baffled, blindsided.

"Well, I don't know about *that*," said Barry. "But I did have a friend whose grandmother's name was Wanda. We spent a week at her house in the country one summer – actually, it must have been a farm. There were some cows, I think, and chickens. We ate these perfect little tomatoes right off the vine . . ."

Holt crouched against the pool wall, pushed off, and glided as far as he could before he began to sink. Then he continued to propel himself away from Wanda and Barry with huge, splashy kicks.

———

The hot tub was full. Holt gripped the handrail and eased in slowly, pausing on each step to acclimatize to the startling temperature. A young woman shifted onto her boyfriend's lap to make room for him. Holt nodded thank you and took his seat across from Fabio. In order to avoid the painful sight of Fabio's nipples, Holt closed his eyes and recalled the touted healing properties of the springs. Apparently, the water was mineral rich: calcium, magnesium, sodium, iron. Holt wondered if a person who soaked long enough might be cured of a deficiency in any one of the minerals, if the anemic or osteoporotic could absorb all that they lacked through their skin.

He opened his eyes and watched the bathers roll their heads from side to side. The heat and effervescence seemed to limber people up; it only made him drowsy. But he'd been tired even before immersing himself, exhausted from the slopes that morning and from the thought of the four-hour bus ride home. Tonight he'd return to Claudette and Beth wouldn't.

"How is she?" his wife had asked the night he'd arrived at the resort, when they spoke before bed.

"Seems fine," Holt said. He thumbed the remote and stopped on a channel that showed several negligee-clad women speaking into phones.

"Isn't it about time we made her come home?" The connection crackled a bit so Holt knew Claudette was in Beth's room, where the jack was loose, on her banana phone.

"I think we've passed that point," he said. "I don't think we can *make* her do anything anymore."

"Smartass," Claudette said. "You know what I mean. We could *ask* her to come home."

The women on the screen tossed their hair. The line swelled with static and fell silent. Holt tried to predict the direction in which their conversation was headed. He couldn't. Within a matter of a minute his wife could be charming and cruel, explosive and kind. It was one of the reasons Holt loved her. It *was* the reason. Whatever Claudette felt, she felt it hugely. But he'd seen how her moods had affected Beth. As a child, Beth had been confused by Claudette's highs and lows. Now she was just pissed off. It seemed to Holt that his wife and daughter had been at odds most of their lives, but drastically so since Beth had transitioned to high school and started skipping classes to hang out downtown. When Claudette went looking for answers, she'd found du Mauriers and butterscotch-flavoured condoms in Beth's purse. Beth couldn't come up with a good excuse for the cigarettes, but the condoms she claimed the school nurse had distributed. Naturally, Claudette got the nurse on the phone. No flavours or colours, the nurse had confirmed. Schools these days dealt only in white latex. Still, Holt believed his daughter when she said she planned to use them as balloons, a hoax for a friend's upcoming birthday party.

A caption flashed at the bottom of the TV screen: *These girls want to talk to YOU!*

"Is she happy at least?" Claudette asked. "Is she having fun?"

"I don't think she minds that I'm here."

"No," Claudette said. "She likes you."

Holt knew it was true. He couldn't think of one instance when he alone had provoked his daughter's ire. But she didn't respect him. And she used him.

"Maybe we shouldn't have given her the option," Claudette said. "To leave, I mean. Maybe that was our mistake."

"Your mistake," Holt said without thinking.

"Mine? Please," Claudette laughed. "You think you're just some bystander in this family?"

"Bingo," he said. While Claudette and Beth threw fits, slammed doors, threatened, he watched from the sidelines, a referee unable to make a call.

"Fuck," Claudette said softly. "I miss her."

"I know," said Holt. "Me too."

Suddenly, he saw that the women on the screen were really girls. He grappled with the remote and killed the power on the TV.

———

As Holt entered the cave, he thought of how they were often analogous to the mouth. Slippery stalactites hung from the roof like tonsils. The calcified walls, ridged and grooved, certainly resembled a palate. He muscled his tongue around inside his mouth, pleased at his observation, which he knew wasn't exactly original.

"Mag-net-head!" someone cheered. It sounded like Barry's kid, but it could have been any one of the boys. Laughter ricocheted through the cave. Holt paused in the waist-deep water and turned so that he could see outside. He was mildly claustrophobic, but he reminded himself that he couldn't get lost; the tunnel was shaped like a horseshoe, with both entrances off the hot tub, and there would only be a second, as he rounded the bend, when he wouldn't be able to see outside. He drew in a few full, steamy breaths through his nose. Cleansing breaths, Claudette called them. Across the deck, in the warm pool, Holt thought he could see Wanda lying across Barry's outstretched arms, the way you'd hold a kid you're teaching to swim.

He waded deeper into the cave, which was lit solely by murky, underwater beams. There were pockets with natural shelves off the main loop and twice he passed couples knotted up in them. He felt like a spectator at a peep show. This was no place for a kid. He thought of the sepia photo hung at the elevator landing and longed for that muted, gentler time. But there was no going back. Some guy, indeed. Holt had bought the beer for the kids. He'd picked up a flat. Beth had asked him sweetly yet forcefully and he'd made her promise they'd stay in their rooms. It was stupid of him, but he'd thought they might not even drink it. He'd hoped they wouldn't like the taste.

Holt sank into the water and crawled forward on his fingertips, with only his head exposed.

"Sssssss," he hissed as he rounded the scoop of the horseshoe.

"What's that?" one of the kids said.

"Ssssssss," Holt hissed again.

"It's a venomous snake," Holt heard Beth say, flatly. He couldn't see her yet.

Last night, he'd identified his daughter amid the rank chaos of the hotel room, huddled on the floor. He hadn't seen her at first because she was cocooned between boys. They'd shed like flimsy skins at his approach.

"Everyone out," Holt said, looking down at his daughter. "Party's over." A few kids went obediently for the door.

"That's a good look for you," Beth said. She was referring to his robe and sneakers.

Holt tightened the belt. "Flattery will get you everywhere," he said, trying to play it cool. Beth rolled her eyes. Holt rolled his. Then he turned and knelt to check magnet-head's pulse. He recognized the girl, Mariko was her name. As kids, she and Beth had coordinated weekend sleepovers. Holt even knew that the scar on Mariko's left cheek, crescent-shaped and white, was the tragic mark of a falling food processor blade that, at one time, and never again, hung on the inside of their pantry door.

"All right," said Holt. "Who's gonna tell me what happened here?"

Mariko groaned and rolled onto her side.

"What does it look like," Beth deadpanned.

Holt picked up a crushed can and tossed it at her. "Were you chucking these at Mariko's head?"

"*She's* the one who passed out," said a normally shy girl, lippy with intoxication.

Another girl sputtered, "She's got this, like, magnetic field around her head!"

"I see," said Holt. On the bedside table he counted a few bottles of liquor that he hadn't purchased. Peach schnapps, sambuca, Malibu.

"You gonna tell Mom?" Beth asked.

"Don't know," said Holt. "You?"

"It sort of depends."

"Right," said Holt. He slid his arms beneath Mariko's back and knees and ratcheted her up off the floor. The girl's eyes blurted open and closed.

"Hey," Beth said. "What are you doing?" She scuttled to block Holt's path from the room. "She's fine! It was just a joke. Leave her here!"

But Holt knew he couldn't leave Mariko in his daughter's care. What if she choked on vomit? What if they tormented her some more? He had to take her to Wanda's room.

"Move," said Holt.

Beth stood with her legs triangled before the door.

"As if," she said.

Silently, Holt counted to ten. "Okay, move now," he said. He used Mariko's limp feet to try to nudge his daughter aside, but Beth held her ground. Holt wasn't normally the one to engage in showdowns with his daughter. He realized that, for once, he might be experiencing Claudette's point of view. For no reason, he thought of that old phrase, *the lady of the house*. It was never *ladies*. Maybe Beth would never return home.

"You know," Holt said, "you've really messed up this time."

"Uh, no," Beth said. "That would be *you*."

"Okay, so we're tied," Holt said, the girl growing heavy in his arms. "Now please get the fuck out of my way."

He didn't say it with conviction; he said it with fatigue. Regardless, it had the pleasing effect of wiping Beth's face clean of its sneer. Like a damp cloth to sponge food from a baby's mouth. Free of expression, Holt was able to see that Beth's features looked large, swollen. It might have been the alcohol, but it was also her age. She was growing into herself. Her nose was too big for her face. Her eyes seemed to open dangerously wide. She looked weird, imposturous. She stood aside.

Holt manoeuvred Mariko through the door frame and began down the hall toward the elevator landing, its purgatorial arrangement of table and chairs.

Now he felt dizzy and outside of himself as he swam in among the group of kids. The water wasn't just hot, it was infernal. He longed for the POLAR BEAR PLUNGE! But it wasn't only the shock of the cold he craved. He wanted to experience the pressure of the waterfall itself, that great obliterating gallonage on his skull.

Holt spotted Beth and crawled toward where she sat, no, where she was throned on a rock shelf. And what if she never came home?

He knelt before his daughter's long, child's legs.

"Don't worry," Beth said, raising her right hand as if to address her followers. "He's harmless."

Then she looked down at Holt. "What do you want," she said. "I'm right here."

# OSCAR MARTENS

## BREAKING ON THE WHEEL

At night Dana can see Winnipeg from the top of the Ferris wheel, not the actual buildings but light reflected off a ceiling of clouds. During the day she can see for miles and each time she reaches the top, she strains to delay her descent toward the mediocrity of ground level, the gas station, her father standing at the controls, yelling at her to smile.

Smiling is important because if people see her smiling and realize how much fun it is, everyone will want to take a ride. Dana is the only one riding, just like yesterday and the day before. When this thing gets going she can give up her seat to a *paying* customer. She doesn't mind helping but she wonders how long it will be before people realize how much fun it is.

There's a brown crust of burned corn forming on the bottom of the pot. Dana can't smell it but she knows she forgot to turn the heat down before she came out to help her father. It would take two minutes to run back to the house, turn it down, and run back, but Bob's not interested.

– Let it burn, we have a business to run.

She's slung to the top again, while her mother sits in the kitchen, every curtain in the house drawn closed.

On Saturday a silver BMW came in for gas and an oil check. The mother seemed so uncomfortable touching anything that was dirty or had the potential to be dirty that Bob did it all for her, even though his was a self-serve station. Her child shyly approached the Ferris wheel and Dana could tell, even from a distance, that the girl was about her age. If she had been on the ground she might have been able to make a new friend.

Her tank full, the mother went to retrieve her child with Bob close behind. She looked at the wheel the same way she had looked at the gas pump: dirty or potentially dirty. Bob noticed the sharp crease in her pants and thought how strange it was that some clothes looked expensive and others didn't, even though they were often made of the same stuff.

– Five bucks.

The mother was startled. She grabbed her girl by the shoulder and directed her toward the car.

– No, two fifty. Five bucks for you *and* the kid.

He stood directly between them and the car, his body stiff, but did not pursue her when she guided her child around him. From Dana's seat she saw them group together briefly, then split apart. The girl glanced back at Dana, following the circle she cut in the air.

Bob had thought he knew what he needed to know about business but over the past eight months he's been learning a whole lot more. Most people would rather pull over for gas at the intersection of 332 and the Trans-Canada. Most people would rather do that than turn right on a service road exit and follow that for half a mile until they got to Bob Hascall's gas station, locally owned and operated. They'd rather go to the Esso and duck into Tim Horton's to get a couple of maple-dipped donuts, or maybe a soup and sandwich, on their way to hell and gone.

The Esso hasn't been there long but it sure has been a punch in the guts for Bob. He's taken to advertising as a way of regaining lost business. There's a spray-painted banner that reads CHEAP GAS on a plywood sheet, propped up in the ditch just before the turnoff. For the past three weeks, just after closing, he's been edging the sign closer to the road. It's halfway into the shoulder now, almost close enough to make contact with traffic. Below CHEAP GAS, in slightly smaller letters, Bob has added FUN FARE.

On Sunday a green van skidded to a stop and when the sliding door opened, a bunch of teenagers jumped out. They were dressed in shorts and Dana could see an inflated inner tube in the back along with a couple of coolers. Lake Winnipeg, she guessed, or maybe a party on the riverbank.

The loud one, red-haired and skinny, was chasing the fat one with a can that squirted dry chemical goo. The driver blasted the horn while the two were in front, wrestling for control of the can. It looked like the same kind of fun promised in beer commercials. Not everyone was beautiful but there was a lot of laughing and screaming and everyone was in on it. The skinny one became winded from his pursuit and bent over with his hands on his knees, gasping for air. In a sideways glance he caught sight of Dana on her metal bench.

She was smiling as instructed but he didn't smile back. He shielded his eyes with his hand to see her more clearly. Her smile was now on maximum voltage, her teeth hurting from the pressure, her cheeks beginning to ache.

Silently she was thinking, FUN, FUN, FUN, FUN, hoping the kids would pick up her vibe. Everyone looked at her and fell silent. The sight of her had broken their fun. Dana smiled harder. One of the girls tugged the arm of the skinny one who eventually turned back to the van. As they drove away, Dana looked down between her feet and felt slightly ill. She had power but it was a horrible power, the power to drive people away. She wished the mounts of the wheel would break so she could roll out of the yard, over the road, into the wheat field, the wheel acting like a giant swather, stalks of grain pulled up and sent flying.

The corn burns while Doris sits at the table in a darkened kitchen, using up oxygen, taking up space, being crushed by the weight of everyday events. She scrapes together the strength to stand, walks over to the cupboard, and grabs two cans, two possible directions for dessert: a can of peaches or a can of pineapple. Peaches or pineapple. Peaches are nice. Pineapple is also nice. They're both nice. They're both in cans. And the cans are the same size.

The horrid smell of the corn is noted but not connected to herself or any action she might take. After lunch Dana used "supper" as many times as she could in her monologue to Doris, hoping her mother would not try to serve Rice Krispies again.

The old Mom is held in the yellow plastic recipe box. When Dana wants to visit her mother as she used to be, she reads the notes written next to recipes: "Double this if Bill is coming over!!" or "Don't serve if Susan is coming. She can't digest raw cucumbers!" Every comment came with a joy that could not be expressed in mere words. Exclamation points and smiley faces marked every instance of superfluous glee.

It arrived on the back of a flatbed truck. Someone was going to throw it away. Bob thought throwing away working machinery was like throwing away money. Some low-life operator couldn't make a go of it, but being a low-life, he probably lacked the necessary work ethic.

The driver paused after he had laid down the last beam and secured the Hiab crane on the back of his truck. The area where the picnic bench used to be was covered in metal frames and girders.

– You want some help putting this thing together? I've got a buddy who's done stuff like this a couple of times before.

– No. You've been paid. You can go.

After the driver left, Bob explained to Dana that organization was the key to success in any project. They spent hours flipping beams end for end, looking at the joints, rearranging the frames before he located a good starting point. By that time Dana's school shirt had a band of grease smeared across it but luckily Bob was focused on other things.

The first joint turned out to be "sticky." Bob started with a socket wrench and some Liquid Wrench, noodling around for almost half an hour, spraying the joint, testing it with the wrench. He sent Dana for the vice grip and a pry bar. Later he asked for the sledgehammer. He hammered on the pin, while Dana held it straight, using all her strength, the vibrations from each blow working their way through her hands, to her elbows and shoulders.

The scientific method finally blew apart and he began to rage on the joint, beating it to death with the sledge. Sparks flew off the metal as Dana backed away from Bob's sweat and swears. All she wanted to do was go back inside, away from him, away from the mosquitoes that seemed to be frenzied by his heavy breathing. Toward 9:00 p.m. she thought she could edge away, back to the comfort of the house in time for *Buffy the Vampire Slayer* but he spotted her going AWOL and ordered her back, if only to be witness to his misery.

A full night's sleep didn't make him any smarter. He needed Bill.

They take their first customers on Monday. The boy's out of the pickup before it stops. His grandfather trails behind. He runs to Bob's side and watches Dana go round and round. Bob, sensing a sale, pushes the throttle down on the coughing engine and a trail of black smoke comes out the stack. The wheel is now turning at top speed. Grandpa returns to the truck and wipes splattered bugs from the windshield with a very dirty squeegee, expecting the boy to follow, but sometimes it's easier to give in to the child's demands, and how could he not, after seeing the boy's face.

They ride in the car just before Dana. After a couple of turns the boy looks back and once he has started he can't stop. She smiles at the back of his head, ready for the next chance to show him how much fun she is having. Her power takes away a little joy every time he turns around. First he looks uncertain, then concerned. After a few more turns he looks like he is going to cry. Grandpa doesn't notice the boy's rigid grip on the handlebar. Bob props his cheeks up with his index fingers to remind Dana but it's too late for charms. Her power has broken the boy. They'll soon go and they won't be back.

Bill came over the morning after Bob's tantrum. It was early, before Dana had even started breakfast and she came out to greet him. There was still dew on the grass but the birds had been singing for hours. He smiled and put his hand on her shoulder as they walked around the pile of beams and girders. She showed him the joint that had finished off Bob's patience. Bill clucked his disapproval as his fingers traced over stripped threads, dents, bright metal exposed where paint had chipped off. He winced at the bent struts that led to the hub. His voice was only loud enough to be heard above the birds. She leaned closer to catch every soft word.

Bill coaxed and jiggled, welded and greased until the thing started to take shape. Bob came out after breakfast and they worked silently until they ran out of sun. They stopped briefly for the food trays Dana brought, then continued working by the headlights of Bill's truck.

The next morning Bob tied one of the stays to his trailer hook and slowly pulled the thing up. He left the truck in park and walked to where Bill was adjusting the far stay.

– You can go now, Bill.

– Why don't I stick around until we're sure she runs?

– You're not getting a cut. Just 'cause you helped put a few joints together doesn't mean you're entitled to anything.

– I don't . . .

– Don't think you're going to worm in on my business. I knew you were going to pull something like this. Just go.

Bill shook his head as he hefted his tools and his welder into the back of the truck. He winked at Dana and cocked his head for her to follow. He had something for her in the glove compartment.

– And don't be giving her any more stuff. She has enough stuff.

Bill wheeled around and nodded to Bob while he held his cupped hand behind his back. Dana took the carved wooden bird and slipped it into her pocket before her father could approach. Bill drove off and winked at Dana as she waved.

The man who stared at her on Tuesday had a careful, deliberate manner. He grasped the nozzle firmly, grounded the metal against the edge of the fill pipe, and pushed it in slowly until the rubber spill stopper was snug. He noticed Dana as the tank filled and after he paid Bob he walked to the foot of the wheel to watch her. She smiled but thought it was doomed. Why would a grown man want to go on a Ferris wheel? She smiled anyway. She wondered if she was too ugly to make other people smile. Why else would no one smile back when they looked up at her, having so much fun, all through the skin-frying day and into the mosquito-ridden night.

When she was close to the ground he mouthed the words, *Are you okay?* She nodded enthusiastically. It seemed possible that her classmates were enduring hellish summers of their own, shovelling mountains of pig manure or stringing barbed wire along fence posts. Possible but not likely. She wanted him to go so he could remember her as the fun-loving smiling girl. She wanted him to go because she couldn't hold back the tears much longer.

Lightning strikes and she counts off the miles. Six, seven, eight, nine . . . it's still a long way off. After an hour of watching the sky grow dark, her father will no longer be able to ignore the storm. In the next two turns or so, the wheel will slow and he will let her off. By the end of five turns, that will be it. Ten turns. Twenty-five turns and another lightning strike, six seconds away. At forty-seven turns her count drifts off, but then the wheel slows and stops just short of the point where she can easily get off. Bob runs to the house and comes back with her clear plastic rain cape. He throws it up to her and starts up the wheel again.

Hard rain turns to hail. The engine cuts out, runs for a bit, then dies completely. Bob runs to the station for a bucket of diesel. Inevitably, the wheel stops with Dana at the highest point. Without the noise and vibration from the engine, she can feel the whole thing twist in the gusts. Rickety. The stays look thin as they go tight then slack with the wind. She considers two deaths: one quick and hot, the other involving a friend from school seeing this.

If she could scream loud enough, maybe Mom would get off the chair. Maybe she'd make the trip a hundred miles from the chair to the window to lift her hundred-pound arms and part the curtain. The sight of her girl on a giant lightning magnet might compel her to grab a coat from the hook and come outside to scream at Bob. Would he listen to her? Would he see her? Would he even understand what was wrong?

Dana closes her eyes. She knows she wouldn't see or hear the strike, but she would see the charge leader, the tiny but inevitable prelude to a strike. Her head bowed, the hood of the raincoat sticks to the clammy skin on the back of her neck.

Sharon lays the map on the hood of the car using her forearms to pin it down against the wind. The ground is still wet but she's glad; the farmers could use the rain. Dark clouds clear as fast as they came on and the sun picks up where it left off. Bob Hascall's Gas Bar is the only address given. She wonders if the house is part of the gas station or located nearby.

The man who called from the pay phone told her a confusing story about an amusement park ride but wouldn't leave his name. She doesn't like starting files on the basis of anonymous sources calling from pay phones. Raymond is silent on the passenger's side. He's not what she'd call athletic but he's a two-hundred-pound guy. He'll do.

Sharon does not like dealing with suspicion and fear. Or standing at the screen door and waiting for someone to come. Sharon does not like the way farms always have a range of lethal weapons at hand. She thinks of a single rifle bullet popping through the aluminum frame of the screen door, entering her liquid-filled guts, deforming into a mushroom shape, then splattering out of her back and into Raymond. But mostly, Sharon does not like the way her vision is obscured by the screen door, as she looks into the dark room behind it, straining to see what's there.

# NAOMI K. LEWIS

## THE GUIDING LIGHT

**G.** Virginia Morgan and I are eating an early lunch at the Tex Mex Annex in Tucson when she tells me, for the first but not the last time, that she's having a very strange week. When I first met her a day ago, her hair was immaculately styled. Today, it is unbrushed and bright red against her green T-shirt, which features a saguaro cactus, a setting sun, and a single orange word, *Oracle*. In the dim light of the wood-panelled restaurant her eyes are almost black, though out in the sun they were an unusually reddish brown. Her nose and cheeks are flushed with sunburn. "Look at my hands," she says, and holds them out. "I had them chemically peeled." The skin is flawless and I tell her so. She sits back, pushing out her full, sun-chapped bottom lip, as she tends to do when displeased. "I'm not foolish," she tells me. "I know what you think of me, and it really doesn't matter in the slightest bit."

Whatever I might think of her, and however dishevelled she may appear at this moment, Ms. Morgan is known for self-possession, both in her manner and in her writing. For fans, her books and "workshops" represent a welcome alternative to psychotherapy and psychoanalysis, allegedly without what she calls the "cultish herd mentality" of other such movements. What her admirers call refreshing clarity, her critics call dim-witted simplicity. Sceptics dismiss and disdain her as just another pop-philosopher getting rich off the misery and gullibility of others.

Ms. Morgan's mantra, which she recommends her readers say out loud in times of stress, is "Forget it." But the first time I saw her, in the Arrivals lounge of the Tucson airport, the day before our tamale lunch, she looked like the kind of person who wouldn't forget anything. She was efficiency personified. She glanced at me with my cardboard sign and bombarded a path straight through the other weary-looking travellers. Her hair was long, auburn, perfectly sleek and straight. Her makeup was immaculate, her beige linen suit unwrinkled, and she strode on black high heels, pulling a suitcase carelessly, as though it were light as a feather. Her appearance was next to miraculous considering she'd just stepped off a plane. She stopped in front of me. If I hadn't known better, I'd have pegged her as an actor. Her hair and makeup, and the famous nose job, made me think of a soap star. I found myself partly itching to assail her right then and there with the questions I'd prepared, and partly wishing I'd never agreed to do the interview at all. She looked at me in my vest and skirt and cowboy boots, then glanced around, waiting for me to say something. *Forget it*, I wanted to tell her, before dropping the cardboard sign and making a run for it.

"I'm Del Bera from the *Tucson Citizen*," I said. "Welcome to Arizona, Ms. Morgan." I told her I'd be taking her out to

Oracle. "That's where the resort is," I added, when she didn't react. She was silent all the way to the parking lot, only saying, "It was fine," when I asked about her flight. She kept glancing around like she couldn't keep her eyes on one sight for more than a few seconds before finding it tiresome. She somehow made me self-conscious about my truck too, the way she squinted at it and then adopted an air of resignation. When Nick and I agreed to buy a bigger vehicle some seven years ago, I went to the dealership with a picture of a big old van in my head, but came home with a shiny black pickup. I knew Nick would be annoyed at first, but I also knew the truck would win everyone over. It was so much grittier and sleeker than some clunky beige SUV. It was a four-seater, so the boys could sit in the back, and our black Lab, Naomi, could ride outside on the bed. I considered putting G. Virginia Morgan's suitcase out there, but thought better of it and stuck it in the back seat. Ms. Morgan climbed in the passenger side with those high heels; if it'd been me, I'd have broken my neck.

When the newspaper editor, Mary, assigned me the inter-view, she'd said the Canadian self-help guru had studied philosophy, just like me. It's true, I majored in philosophy right in town at U of A, decades ago, before I married Nick and had the boys, and I've often thought back on those courses I took. When Jess and Andrew, my sons, were young and asked me, *why Mom, why, why, why*, I'd think how impossible it was to ever answer that question to any thoughtful folks' satis-faction, and how in the second half of the twentieth century, all a philosophy degree could do was confirm the futility of such an endeavour. In bad faith, I resorted to the long-lived "Because I said so." Or worse, "You'll understand when you're older," as though, come college and adulthood, that opaque shell would peel away, presenting the universe to my boys as a glowing, truthful whole.

Mary gave me copies of all three self-help books. The *About the Author* blurbs didn't tell me much, but they did say G. Virginia Morgan "studied philosophy and psychology" at a college in Canada. But in the course of my research, which I undoubtedly overdid, this being my first assignment as a newspaper interviewer, I discovered Ms. Morgan never graduated from any college; she dropped out before completing the undergraduate degree and never went back. As Missy Vanderos, Ms. Morgan's agent and housemate of the last seven years, told me, "Virginia's a complete bookworm, but prefers learning by herself to discussing that stuff in a classroom setting. I think it's because she's more interested in applying what she reads to real life, instead of writing a bunch of papers that would never see the light of day." I was afraid Ms. Morgan would be one of those touchy-feely counsellor types. We went to one when Jess was twelve and kept getting into fights with this thug at school. The boys' teachers had always called me Mrs. Bera, but the counsellor called me Delilah, and Nick by his first name too, as soon as we entered her office. She referred to Jess as "Jesse." Now, I don't know a lot about psychology, but it seems plain that counsellors ought to be careful to call people by the names they actually go by. If she'd have called us Del and Jess, we might have been more inclined to take her seriously. As it was, she examined my son from his muddy sneakers on up to his most mischievous look, the one where his left eyebrow goes all crooked, and said, "Jesse, you look sad. Can you tell your parents why you're feeling so sad?" Jess met my eyes and grinned wide, all those braces flashing metallic, and I'm sorry to say I joined my son and husband in a good laugh at that counsellor's expense.

But as I headed north on the 77, the self-help writer was quietly high-strung beside me, about as far from touchy-feely as a person can get. She was staying at one of those tacky resorts, those cartoon versions of Arizona set up for northerners whose feet would shrivel if they ever set foot in a real desert, and whose tongues would shrivel just as readily if presented with an unadulterated chili pepper. The resort wasn't in Tucson, but north, just past Oracle. I had asked to pick her up at the airport so I'd be able to get a head start on the interview, a feel for the interviewee as it were. I thought of doing an interview in the first place because I'm known for being pretty good at getting an idea of people, a feel for the way they work. It comes largely from being a mother and a wife – living for twenty years with three men who've never been known to communicate directly. G. Virginia Morgan did not seem eager to converse. I pointed out and named a huge saguaro cactus. "Those are the cacti you usually see in Westerns and such," I explained, "but they actually only grow in this part of the Sonora desert." She looked at the cactus obligingly, squinted out the window and nodded in a falsely contemplative way. "You must be tired," I said. She turned and looked at me, just stared at my face like she wasn't sure who I was and had only just noticed she was in my company. I reminded her about our interview the next afternoon at the resort, and that I'd be attending her workshop in the evening.

She nodded. "Sounds fine."

I'd read about her "workshops." I'd seen a clip of one on TV, so I had some idea of what to expect. Each audience member has to bring an item from her house. It has to be something she's had for a year or more, and that's kept in a corner or a drawer or the back of a closet. Since I was attending the first day of the workshop, I had received the preparatory pamphlet, and had already "excavated" my own "buried burden." It was a good excuse to tidy my desk, going through the drawers looking for something suitable. I chose an unused journal from 1995. It was full of photos of fluffy kittens wearing helmets or aprons and the like, and an inscription inside the cover wished me a merry Christmas from my sister-in-law, Caroline, who hates pets and considers me to be an "animal person." G. Virginia Morgan was right – I'd shoved this journal to the back of the drawer several times over the last five years, pushing it quickly out of sight each time I tidied. *Hold the object for one minute and then write down three words describing how it makes you feel.* Guilty, annoyed, embarrassed. *Would you display this object on your mantle, your coffee table, or your wall?* No. *Then you've excavated a buried burden.* I'd heard about what happens at these workshops – that everyone drops their burdens in a metal bin, and Ms. Morgan invites a volunteer to set it alight. Nick and I have a box of firecrackers in our basement and I wondered what the self-help guru would do if I excavated them for her indoor bonfire. The idea is for each audience member to go home after the workshop and purge her house – excavate and burn everything that she doesn't one-hundred-percent want out in the open. Drawers, closets, and cupboards are certainly useful and probably necessary,

Ms. Morgan admits in *The Willing Amnesiac*, but don't abuse them. Do not hoard.

She stared out the window and I snuck occasional glances at her, looking for evidence of the fact that we were the same age. I noticed crow's feet at the corners of her eyes. Laugh lines, Nick calls mine. I was glad to see them on her. In her author photos, Ms. Morgan looks completely composed and at ease. Like someone who's got it all figured out, and who's got no qualms about whether she's right. Her books are written in the same way – with the kind of confidence I could never pull off in my own college papers. My son Andrew's the same as I am, always getting marks docked for qualifying everything with *it seems to me* and *if I'm not mistaken*. Nothing like that in G. Virginia Morgan's writing.

"I guess you must have jet lag," I offered.

"I'm coming from BC," she said, "so not really."

"I thought Toronto."

"No, I just did a talk in Vancouver." I knew where Vancouver was, right near Washington State. My grandparents came from up there in the Twenties, first came to Arizona because of my grandfather's asthma. They were wealthy folks from Seattle and came for one of the health spas that were opening up around that time. They found the dry air did wonders for Granddad's lungs and wound up settling near Tucson. In Oracle, in fact, just a stone's throw from where Ms. Morgan was staying. All of this would have been obvious conversational fodder, but I kept it to myself. I hate to be one of those folks that rattle on just to fill up air time. Silence truly is golden, a fact that's always escaped Nick and the boys. With Jess and Andrew gone to college, of course, the atmosphere in my house can get a little too golden. It feels eerie to be at no one's beck and call for so many hours of the day, and I laugh at myself for running to Naomi's side with the leash like she's the one letting me out for some air.

"What're those mountains?" said Ms. Morgan.

"The Santa Catalinas." She stared past me, tapping her fingers on her thighs in an odd, rhythmic manner, one hand faster than the other. Her nails were long and shiny, a glossy see-through pink, and she occasionally interrupted her finger-tapping with a flurry of slaps, whole palm against her leg, as though she were brimming over with anticipatory anxiety. It was around then that I caught my reflection and unclipped the barrette I'd spent so long over that morning, letting my hair spring upwards in all its curly mayhem. I wanted to rub off the ridiculous-looking red lipstick I'd applied, but figured rubbing my mouth on the back of my hand would be even less dignified than letting my lips stay shiny like a kid's after a popsicle. I tossed the barrette over my shoulder onto the back seat, which I'd vacuumed of Naomi-hair just for G. Virginia Morgan. We drove the rest of the way in silence.

The resort was some fifteen minutes off the highway, at the end of a road lined with manicured-looking palm trees. We stopped by the front entrance of what looked like a palatial adobe hut. Smaller casitas spotted the terrain, and miles of saguaro-spotted golf course sprawled out to meet the horizon. I didn't bother to park properly, just left the engine running. I lifted G. Virginia Morgan's suitcase out of the truck and made a show of dusting it off. A young man in an official-looking uniform came over with his hands clasped in front of him. "Ms. Morgan?" he said. Driving home, I almost convinced myself not to show up the next day, especially when I noticed my notebook lying open on the dashboard, my most obnoxious interview questions right in what had been Ms. Morgan's line of vision.

That night, I opened my desk drawer again and reconsidered my choice of "burden" for torching the next day. I've always kept some mementos that the average person might consider peculiar. I have a whole shoebox of such oddities right in my desk, and I knew that G. Virginia Morgan would want me to rid myself of them all. For example, I've never told Nick this, but I have the package that contained my first twenty-eight birth control pills, from back in the Seventies in LA. It's an embarrassing thing to have stashed away, and truly, I would not display it on my coffee table. When I held it in my hand, like Virginia's pamphlet instructed, and considered how it made me feel, I have to confess I didn't feel much of anything at all. It was such a long time ago. There was a soap opera actor I was sort of mildly in love with at the time. In any case, I reconsidered disposing of that old plastic wrapper, and wondered at my motives for keeping it. But I ended up sticking it back in the shoebox. I took the kitty journal out, so I wouldn't forget it in the morning.

The next day was Saturday, the day of the interview. I was supposed to be back at the resort for eleven to interview Ms. Morgan over lunch, then relax for a few hours while she had some time to herself, and finally attend her workshop in the evening. It's only an hour's drive, but I set out at nine forty-five, being too nervous and jittery to sit around the house any longer. This time I did my hair and mascara the usual way, and wore a long, flowered dress with a blazer and my cowboy boots. Nick handed me a cup of coffee for the road and said I'd be fine; Naomi followed me to the door and I rumpled her ears, told her to wish me luck, then set out.

When I got out on the highway, the sun was glaring like crazy, so I put on my sunglasses. I felt kind of proud of my surroundings, the way you do when you have a guest from away. The mountains, the dusty desert, the cacti, all took on an exotic aspect as I tried to imagine being from Toronto, Canada, with its snow and packed-in buildings and below-zero temperatures. There weren't many cars on the road and there was a kind of peacefulness that calmed me right down. The coffee swished through my veins and into my brain, bringing its usual rush of optimism. I rehearsed my interview questions in my head, starting with the easiest, lightest ones and wondered if I'd make it to the stuff I was really curious about.

I drove past the Coronado National Forest, pointing out the foliage to an imaginary G. Virginia Morgan in my head. *Those are cottonwood trees and over there's one of the biggest saguaros I've seen.* She was much more interested in my narrative than the real woman had been the day before. *My granddad says when he moved here from Washington State, he thought the cactus flowers must've been fake and glued on.* I pictured her confiding in me about some family history of her own, which she'd already done in real life by writing those books, and I fell into contemplation over how long it'd been since I'd had a girlfriend – someone to shoot the breeze with.

I was halfway to Oracle when I spotted a hitchhiker way up ahead of me – just a dot of colour against the reddish-brown landscape. It's not usual to see someone walking on the road, and I wondered if I should pick the person up, make sure he or she got into Oracle before midday, when the sun would be at its hottest and highest. As I neared though, I realized the woman wasn't hitchhiking at all. For one thing, she was headed in the wrong direction – walking south on my side of the highway – and she completely ignored the one car ahead of me, not sticking out her thumb or even turning her head. She was walking quite a distance from the road as well, in the dirt beyond the shoulder. I wondered if her car was broken down a ways back, and if she was trying to walk to a service station. She had her head down, so it was only as I drove by and she looked up, squinting, that I realized. In fact, it took me a few seconds to absorb the information and stop the car, because it seemed so unlikely. But I was sure of it – the highway walker was G. Virginia Morgan. She was wearing dark blue jeans and a baggy, bright green Oracle T-shirt, a black sweater tied around her waist. If she walked all that way in a pair of thongs, which she'd clearly done, her feet must have been killing her. I noticed she wasn't carrying anything, not even a purse or a bottle of water. Her hair had lost its sleekness and was curling frizzily at the tips, the way over-dyed hair tends to.

I did a U-turn onto the shoulder of the road and drove slowly past her. Opening my window, I took off my sunglasses, secured them on top of my head, and looked back at her. She was still walking toward me. Virginia's skin looked flushed and hot. "You're getting a bad burn," I called out to her. Then, wondering if she remembered me at all, I added, "We were supposed to meet at eleven?" She stopped, arms crossed, to look at me inscrutably. "Listen," I said, "that's shaping up to be a bad burn. I've got some cold cream in the truck. If you get in, I can take you where you need to be."

She wasn't wearing a stitch of makeup, and there were a few freckles across the bridge of her nose, and on her forehead and chin, like you'd expect to see on someone much younger. She took a step back and glanced over her shoulder, as though she was planning on making a run for it, away from the road. An absurd picture popped into my head, of me chasing the self-help guru across the dusty plain. What would I do when I caught up? Tackle her? Pin her down and scream interview questions? "That's going to be painful," I said, fixating on the sunburn as fodder for persuasion. "You've got to get out of the sun." I leaned over and pushed the passenger door wide open, regretfully turning my back on her for a few seconds. "Climb in," I told her, like it was the most normal thing in the world to find an interviewee wandering down the highway a three-hour walk from our meeting place. She shaded her eyes with a manicured hand, and I saw that she'd cut her nails short, the same length as my own. To my relief, she walked around in front of the truck and climbed in.

I handed her my big water bottle from under the seat and she immediately drained a quarter of it, stopped to breathe hard, and then took another swig. Put the bottle between the seats. "You want me to take you back to the resort?" I asked. She shook her head, furrowing her almost non-existent eyebrows and turning to glance south down the road. I checked for traffic and changed lanes, headed back the way I'd come. I kept glancing over at Ms. Morgan – she looked about a hundred times better without makeup. Of course, she was beginning to look a bit like a lobster, especially under the eyes. But her face was real pretty. Sweaty though, and her full, red lips were cracking. I was afraid she was dehydrated, and was relieved by the way she kept taking swigs from the water bottle.

"You're lucky I picked you up," I told her. "In an hour from now, it'll be a whole lot hotter out here. You'd better get some sunscreen and a water bottle if you're planning on doing any more walking around. And a good hat. And a good pair of shoes." I recalled what I'd told her the day before when she clearly wasn't listening – how a lot of people make the mistake of heading out into the desert this time of year, thinking it isn't too hot so they'll be fine. But even when it's fairly cool, the sun's a killer. It was an effort not to lecture her further – to try and make her understand the peril she'd put herself in, breaking every rule of desert safety. Growing up in these parts, it's drilled into your head from birth. Don't walk in the desert by yourself, or without telling anyone where you're headed, or without a hat and sunglasses, or wearing dark colours. And the number one rule, don't walk out to the middle of nowhere with no way of getting back. I was sure she knew nothing about snakes or scorpions either. Must've been my maternal instinct coming out; half of me was relieved to have found her in time, and half of me wanted to throttle her for being so careless with her own well-being.

Handing over the bag of salted peanuts from my purse, I explained, "You might need salt. Your body loses sodium from sweating, and from drinking all that water. Next time you use the restroom, you'll likely lose half your electrolytes." She took the bag out of my hand and reached in for a couple of nuts. I had the sense she'd do anything I told her. I was aware of speaking to her like she was much younger than me, instead of almost the same age. A woman in her late forties.

"Where were you headed to?" I asked. She looked at me, still squinting from the sun's glare. "Are you still doing your workshop tonight, at the resort?"

She sighed heavily, put a hand to her forehead, and looked up as though hoping for divine intervention. "Shit," she said. "Motherfucking goddamn shit." She continued to shade her eyes, so I opened the glove compartment again and retrieved Nick's aviator sunglasses. I had to laugh when she put them on. She checked herself out in the mirror and said, "Ha! I look like a fly. Thanks, Del." I was more than surprised she remembered my name; I'd been certain she didn't remember me.

I headed back past Coronado. It was plain that Virginia had either been walking aimlessly or didn't want to tell me where she was trying to go. I asked if she wanted to go to the hospital and she shook her head vehemently. She didn't seem physically ill, and I had no way of knowing what she was usually like. I asked if she was hungry and she replied, "Starving."

"I'll take you someplace for lunch," I told her. I used what Nick calls the voice of no return. I've perfected it over the years – it allows no possibility of argument from a child that hears it. Of course, Virginia wasn't a child. But she didn't argue.

It was during that drive back into Tucson that I decided to write a magazine article alongside the short interview for the newspaper. I'd already gone overboard on my research, tracking down and phoning all of Virginia's relatives. Most of the people I called were surprisingly willing to speak with me, except for Virginia's ex-husband, who never returned any of my calls. I'd read all three of her books, and gone on to read something by each author she referenced, including Nietzsche, Spinoza,

Frankl, and Wiesel. Nick thought I'd lost my mind, kept reminding me I was only supposed to write a thousand words. In fact, Nick tried to dissuade me from tracking down those relatives of hers, pointing out that she'd changed their names in the books for a reason. "Well, if they don't want to talk to me," I told him, "they don't have to." It was easy enough to seek them out, and I felt like an investigative reporter on the case.

Nick was already annoyed just by my reading those self-help books and talking about G. Virginia Morgan's philosophy over dinner.

"Why are you wasting your time on this schlock?" he said. So I didn't let him know how much more time I wasted after that. He could tell I was getting obsessive and seemed to take it personally, like he was afraid I might run off with G. Virginia Morgan into the Canadian sunset.

"This is my first interview," I told Virginia. She looked at me, leaning her cheek against the back of her seat, so I kept talking. "I planned on being a writer back when I finished college, but it didn't pan out." I told her how I moved to LA at the age of twenty-two, thinking I'd write for TV. It was a disillusioning year. Enlightening, but nothing like what I'd pictured. First of all, Hollywood is just about the least glamorous place you could hope to visit, unless your idea of glamour involves a lot of fluorescent lights, pizza joints, and bingo. Picture living inside an amusement park, surrounded by badly dressed tourists and those awful people who've been on the edge of fame for the last twenty years and figure they're going to be a star any day now. I got a job working for a soap opera. My grandmother had been watching *Guiding Light* since it started about a million years ago – she even listened to it on the radio in its early days – and she liked to think I was writing for them. She'd call me and ask what the characters were like in person. She was pretty old at that point, and showing signs of dementia. But I actually worked for a show called *Dangerous Lives*. This was the late Seventies, but the show was ahead of its time and the characters had an oddly Eighties, get-ahead-at-all-costs feel that I could only pinpoint in retrospect. I aspired to be a writer, but my job was actually reading the fan mail. I attended story meetings to report on general trends in the letters. If the viewers were all upset about the way a story was going, or wanted two characters to break up or get together, then the writers would incorporate those plot lines.

"There was a religious undertone in the show," I told Virginia. "The characters were always asking God why He was inflicting such torments upon them. It was strange to think that there was a force influencing their lives, but instead of God, it was those wacky letter-writers, driven to pen-and-paper by the plights on their TV screens. The thing they seemed to like most was to watch an innocent, likeable character driven to the edge of destruction by her evil nemesis, only to be rescued from the very brink of death."

"Imagine if life were really like that," said Virginia. She ate a few more peanuts, apparently imagining it herself. "Ha!" she said. "So is that why dead characters are always coming back to life?"

"Sometimes," I told her. "Characters would come back after being dead for five years. They'd be played by a different actor. The writers just explained it all away with amnesia and plastic surgery." She didn't react. It occurred to me that amnesia and plastic surgery were major themes in Virginia's books. Maybe she was not so much like a soap star, I mused, as a soap character.

Once we reached town, I automatically headed for my favourite restaurant, the Tex Mex Annex. They make a good tamale, and they let dogs in, so I go there pretty frequently when I want a bite out by myself – Naomi curls up under the table and I settle in with a good read, something spicy to eat, and a cold drink. It's not what you'd call a classy joint, but it's got plenty of local flavour; and they use good ingredients – no skimping on the peppers and not a trace of Velveeta to be seen. The restaurant's above a bookstore, and Virginia followed me up the narrow, wooden staircase. The Tex Mex Annex is really in a sort of attic, with high, slanted, wood-panelled walls and exposed wooden crossbeams.

The waitress brought us water and tortillas with salsa right away. The best medicine for a tired, misguided highway-hiker, I assured myself, watching her drain a glass of water and steadily gobble half a basket of chips. Finally, she licked her fingers and sighed. "I'm not usually like this. I'm having a very strange week." Now she frowns down at her T-shirt, shaking her head. "So," she says, crossing her arms on the table and sitting up straight. "Are you going to interview me or what?"

G. Virginia Morgan was born Gabriele Virginia Reilly in Ottawa, Canada, in 1953. Her mother and grandmother, Dutch Jews, had emigrated from the Netherlands to Canada after the Nazis obliterated the rest of their family during the Second World War. Virginia's father was Irish-Canadian, and died when Vee, as he called her, was nine. From then on, she was raised by her mother and grandmother, and was known to all as Ginny. For Virginia's readers, this is a familiar story: the oppressive closeness of her household compelled her to move in with a boyfriend in 1975, when she was twenty-two. Ginny's first daughter, Agnes,* was born nine months later, but not before the boyfriend left the country, never to be seen again. Three years later, Ginny married, and in 1986 her daughter Jessica was born. For the next five years, Ginny taught piano lessons, read in her free time, and as Virginia writes in *The Willing Amnesiac*, "existed rather than lived, in a monotonous routine remarkable only for its lack of any distinguishing features." In 1991, when she was thirty-eight, Ginny fell down a flight of stairs and hit her head. She suffered from temporary amnesia, and her personality was permanently altered. After a year, she decided to change her name, leave her family, and start a new life. Since then, she has lived with her agent and best friend, Missy Vanderos; the pair own houses in Spain and Toronto. With Ms. Vanderos's help, Virginia has written and published three successful self-help books, appeared on numerous talk shows, and travelled North America with her message. Her philosophy is self-described as "laughter in the faces of those who'd like to see us break down and cry in public." Indeed, Virginia disdains most self-help practitioners, as well as psychologists and the like, who advocate exposure of past suffering to heal the scars it has allegedly left on the psyche. Virginia asserts in her first and most

---

* Not her real name. Virginia Morgan uses pseudonyms for all her relatives in her books, so I've used the same names as she does.

successful book, *The Willing Amnesiac*, that "dirty laundry should be washed, not aired; and if still stained, it should be burned to ashes." Virginia's present surname, Morgan, is of her own devising. When I ask how she chose it, she smiles. "Sometimes a name is just a name."

Virginia says I should order for her, so I ask for two tamale lunch specials with a side of mole, thinking the spicy chocolate sauce will be an exotic oddity for a Canadian. While we wait, I ask, "How much do you actually remember from before your head injury?"

"Well," says Virginia, "I remember a lot of things. I sort of remember chunks of my life in a blur, and occasionally a specific event stands out. Comes into my mind clear as day."

"Sounds pretty normal," I venture.

"Yes," she says slowly. "I suppose it does. But before my amnesia, I was constantly going over old memories, specific memories, examining them and torturing myself with them. As though, if I examined them closely enough, I might be able to change them or make their meaning clear. The difference is, I've come to recognize that obsessing over memories is like staring at a wall, waiting for a pattern to emerge. It's a complete waste of time and energy."

"The main effect of your head injury was that your personality changed."

"Yes," acknowledges Virginia. "When my memories came back, I felt like the person who experienced those things was someone other than myself. I'd changed. I didn't feel any connection with the people around me, as though the bonds cemented by a common history had irreparably broken. It was very difficult, and very freeing."

Virginia's mother, known to readers as Teresa, lives in Ottawa, Canada. In her late seventies, she still runs her own aesthetics business. She was reticent when speaking with me on the phone, explaining with the faintest hint of an Eastern European accent that she now has only sporadic contact with her daughter. "For about two years I didn't hear from her at all. Now she phones about once a year. She says she is no longer the same person, and I think it is true. It's a difficult thing." Teresa does, however, have close relationships with both of Virginia's daughters. She hasn't read any of Virginia's books. When I asked why, she quickly ended our conversation.

The tamales come, two each, surrounded by rice, refried beans with melted cheese on top, and a little shredded lettuce. "Seems like I haven't eaten anything but raw vegetables in years," says Virginia, swallowing a mouthful of tamale. "Fucking hell, this is good." She closes her eyes, like a person who's been deprived of food and relaxation for a long time, and doesn't know whether to cry or laugh, savour or gobble, when presented with a proper meal.

"Raw vegetables?"

"My diet. Shakes and veggies, plain chicken breasts some-times. Lean Cuisine. God." I remember the part in her most recent book where she talks about her adolescent weight-gain. Giving way to instinct, she writes, gobbling her grandmother's fattening concoctions and letting the weight of the past coat her bones. She dips a finger in the mole sauce and puts it in her mouth, her sunburned lips closing around it with near-pornographic sensuality. Pulling her finger from her mouth, she drops her head down, forehead on palm so her hair falls around her face. I can see, at the top of her head, where her undyed hair is a more muted colour streaked with grey. Even more grey than my own hair.

"You know why I went on that diet?" she says finally, as though speaking to herself. "It was to lose weight, but also because the taste and smell of food is the only thing that makes me remember, that puts me right back. Even after all these years, biting into spicy food is like pressing my face into my grandmother's fat hands. She made this sauce once." Virginia taps the small, plastic cup containing the mole sauce. "I remember this sauce. I was excited by the idea of eating chocolate for dinner so I smothered my chicken with it. Smothered. Halfway through, it was nauseating, but we had to finish everything on our plates. That was the rule – otherwise my grandmother would cry. She'd get hysterical. I mean, it really wasn't an option at all, not to eat all of it. It felt like my mouth and throat were coated with this sticky, this syrupy layer. So of course I threw up. I went to the bathroom and turned on the fan and the taps, because I didn't want her to hear and know I was wasting food. I made myself eat less than I wanted for the next week to make up for it." She looks at me. "Wasting food was the biggest crime in my house. One time my father spilled salt on the floor and I saw my grandmother sweep it up and put it back in the salt shaker." She pushes her plate away and shakes her head dramatically, looking around as though she's just woken from a dream. I have a peculiar sensation that she is acting. Putting on a one-woman show just for my benefit.

"So you have some pretty emotional memories then," I say.

"I'm having an extremely strange week," sighs Virginia. I'm curious to know just what's so strange about this week in particular, but sense that she doesn't wish to divulge. I take this opening to ask about Virginia's family history, although I know she is opposed to dwelling on such things. I apologize, before I begin, for introducing a topic inherently "irrelevant" according to her own philosophy. "Your mother and grandmother were Holocaust survivors. You mention very briefly, in your first and second books, that your grandmother was actually in Auschwitz and your mother was in hiding for two years. They were reunited after the war?" Virginia nods. "And emigrated to Canada," I add.

"That's right."

"And you mention in *The Maternal Return* that your grandfather and uncle, along with most of your mother's extended family, died in the camps. It's curious to me that you mention this family history so briefly in a book that deals extensively with mother-daughter relationships." As I'm speaking, Virginia digs through the pockets in her black sweater and retrieves a pack of cigarettes. She lights up and looks at me quizzically as she takes a long drag. Apparently, she considers her barely touched meal finished.

"How so?"

"Well, you mention your mother's strange relationship with your grandmother, and how you felt oppressed by their closeness. But you don't really address the fact that they were both terribly traumatized in the war. Do you think that experience might explain an awful lot of their behaviour?" I was going to mention that the Holocaust is pretty much the most obvious example of a historical event that shouldn't, most people would agree, be forgotten, lest it be repeated. In fact, a reviewer in the *Phoenix Sun* mentioned concentration camps to criticize Virginia's "willing amnesia," and he didn't even notice that Virginia's mother and grandmother were Holocaust survivors themselves. And wars, massacres, all sorts of trauma. It seems too simple to just forget about these things in order to get over them. I was also going to bring up the remarkable number of Holocaust writers that Virginia cites in her books, and the fact that her nose job has erased the only feature she shared with the Semitic side of her family. But she speaks before I have a chance to continue.

"I'm absolutely sick of that stuff," she tells me. "You know, there are atrocities and genocides happening every day in this world and there always have been. You're right, families with that kind of history have their own particular neuroses. But it's no excuse. It's no excuse." She smokes her cigarette with uncommon ferocity. "It's like those letters from the soap fans," she tells me. "People get a sado-masochistic kick out of suffering. Out of poking at old wounds, their own and those of others. And inflicting wounds on themselves if no one will do it for them. There's something voluptuous about coming as close to death, as close to absolute horror as conceivably possible and surviving. It incites a sickly envy and excitement in everyone you meet." She exhales smoke through her perfectly straight nose. "Those soap opera letters," she repeats. "Thanks for telling me about that, Del. I'd like to mention them in my next book. It just goes to show that what a lot of people really crave is to observe and contemplate suffering – like a child torturing an insect. Like a public execution. If people were really concerned about the Jewish Holocaust they would be out in the world trying to stop the genocides that are happening today. Not rehashing the past. But anyway, I'm not interested in politics and history. That's really not my thing. I'm interested in people." I don't know how to respond, so we're silent while she finishes her cigarette. I'm about to launch into my next question when she says, looking past me, "Why do you feel like the past is so much more interesting than the present? The past is nothing. It's *gone*. Why do you think you need to know about my family to know something about me? I'll tell you something. These questions you're asking won't tell you a thing about me, because I have nothing to do with all that crap. Let's talk about something else. Ask me something else."

The other topics I'm itching to broach are also tricky. I know I should ask about Virginia's fans, about her travels and her current life. Instead, I say, "You have no contact with your two daughters, and virtually none with your mother." Virginia meets my eyes and holds my gaze, silent, for several seconds. She narrows her eyes and seems about to say something – I'm sure she's about to tell me I just *don't get it* – and then stops with a sharp intake of breath.

"That's right," she says finally. "I do speak to my mother on occasion. I don't have a lot in common with her. As for my daughters and their fathers. Those people are from another life. Another woman's life." Virginia pauses, trying to find the words to make me understand. "It's terrible to lose a parent, I know. And that's what happened; they lost a parent. Their mother doesn't exist anymore. But frankly, that wasn't a whole person, wasn't a person doing anything worthwhile."

"You feel that the world is a better place without the person you used to be."

"That's right. I'm sorry to say it so harshly. But I'm a better person than she was. I'm able to live fully, contribute to the world." She emphasizes her words, waving her hand like a conductor. "I'm a person. I'm a real person."

I tracked down Virginia's older daughter, Agnes, in Toronto, Canada. Although she was born and raised in Ottawa, she now lives in the same city as her estranged mother. The first time I phoned, the twenty-five-year-old told me she had nothing to say about her mother, but surprised me a week later with a message on my answering machine. When I returned her call, I learned she'd moved to Toronto for college over six years ago, and had never run into Virginia. Although Virginia claims her fourteen-year-old daughter lives in Ottawa with her father and stepmother, Agnes told me Jessica is currently living in Toronto, in Agnes's care. "It's a temporary situation," explained Agnes, an unusually articulate young woman. When queried about her mother, her response was similar to Teresa's. "Virginia Morgan is not really my mother," she explained. "In a sense, she is my mother. But in a very tangible way, she is not the same person I knew growing up. After her head injury, her personality completely changed. It wasn't just that she couldn't remember things. She walked differently, talked differently. Used different phrases and liked different books. She didn't feel like she belonged in our family anymore. Obviously, she didn't do it on purpose. It wasn't really her fault."

Yet, in the ironically titled *Accidents*, Virginia insists that most so-called accidents happen for a reason. Whether they happen because of fate or because of unconscious desires is not quite clear – she seems to fluctuate between the two positions. *Accidents* begins with a resonant passage from Nobel Peace Prize–winner Elie Wiesel's short story "The Accident": *"What are we waiting for?" [she asked] . . . "Nothing." I was lying without knowing it. We were waiting for the accident.* In Wiesel's story, a man is hit by a taxi and wakes up hospitalized, in a body cast. Throughout the story, he realizes that he wanted the car to run him over; that he was disappointed to have survived. I ask Virginia, as I drive her back to the resort for her workshop, why she chose a story about suicide as the grounding metaphor for her book.

"No one has asked me that before," she admits. "Well, I think that when we feel cornered, we do look for ways out. That's part of what I'm talking about in my book. We do whatever we can to make a change. Death is just the ultimate change," she says, nodding seriously. "People who attempt suicide don't really want to die. They just don't know how else to change their lives."

"And your own accident?" I venture. "Your head injury?"

"Yes," nods Virginia. "Well, I do think that happened because it was the only way I could change my life. But I don't remember the accident itself."

"You can't remember that day at all," I offer, having read as much in her first book.

"That's right."

It's not even one o'clock by the time I'm driving Virginia back to Oracle, and I finally ask her why she set out walking on the highway that morning. The sun's glaring even worse than in the morning, and she's donned the aviator glasses again.

"If you're in the right frame of mind," she says slowly, "things just fall into place. You just *live*. This morning, I didn't know where I was going, why I felt compelled to buy a T-shirt and shoes at the gift store and start walking. I didn't know why I walked right out of Oracle and kept going for hours.

Consciously, I'd put our interview out of my head, but then there you were. Like it was meant to be that way. I was never in danger, you see. Because you were coming down the road with a bottle of water for me. And if I hadn't set out on that walk, we'd never have gone to the Tex Mex Annex, and I wouldn't have eaten that mole sauce and thought of my grandmother. You see?"

"Uh huh," I agree, skepticism surely evident in my voice.

"I set out on that walk because I felt like it. When I left the resort I didn't know I'd go all the way to the highway. When I reached the road, I had no idea I'd keep going for so long. But I just went; I put all my obligations out of my head. The interview, the workshop. But they're happening anyway, because they were meant to." I can't think of a suitable response, so I keep quiet. "Del," Virginia insists, "that's how my life works. Every day. Every, every day. I just let go, let myself fall, and I end up where I'm supposed to be."

"I think I understand," I tell her, and in a strange sense I think maybe I do. It's easy to get caught up in what she's saying; she looks so darned sure. I mean, I just couldn't ever be one of those New Agey types, talking the way she does. But still, while in her presence, I can see why so many readers fall for her exuberant certainty. It's only thinking of that family of hers that jolts me out of it. The thought of cutting myself off from the boys, Nick, my dad. I just can't fathom it. Just can't see it, ultimately, as anything but a massive shirking of responsibility. It's one thing if you decide not to start a family in the first place. If my own writing career had worked out, I would've stayed in LA, never married Nick, never had the boys. When I was in college, I never really pictured my life turning out the way it has. Something has me wondering lately, for the first time in a long while, what would have happened if I'd stuck it out that year in LA, tried harder to get the kind of job I wanted instead of getting discouraged and getting my heart broken by some actor, and heading back to Tucson. I don't know if it's Virginia who's made me think about these things – honestly, it probably has more to do with the boys moving out and me being in the house all day, daunted by the desire to start a writing career at the age of fifty.

When I broach the topic of responsibility toward other people, Virginia tells me, "We're responsible only for living authentically. You're never doing someone a favour by sacrificing yourself to them – staying with someone out of obligation is an insult to them and to yourself." She asks if she can smoke in the truck and I say yes even though I don't really want her to. She doesn't bother to hold her cigarette outside the open window beside her. "Listen," she says. "The truth is, maybe I did leave the resort this morning because I didn't want to see you." I'm too startled by this revelation to respond, though I can see her face turned expectantly toward me.

"I'm a human being," she says, "with feelings, just like anyone else. Sometimes I behave in ways that seem unreasonable, and only become aware of my motivations later. I was not looking forward to seeing you. Yesterday or today. I'll tell you why. Four days ago now, I was giving a workshop in Toronto. A big one, an audience of around a hundred people. And who do you think was there?" I don't answer. I try to look at her, but only see my own reflection in each side of Nick's sunglasses. They really are too big for her face. "My daughters," she says. "My daughters were both there. Obviously, I recognized them when they came up to the stage with their buried burdens. Guess what their burdens were, Del. Copies of my first book. They each had one."

"Wow," I say. "That must have been. I mean. What did you do?"

"I finished that portion of the workshop, then called a break. I told them we could talk for twenty minutes and then they had to leave. I gave them their workshop fees back of course." She looks at me, waiting for a response, but I don't know what to say. "My daughter told me you called her, Del. She said you'd even called her biological father in California."

"He didn't really say anything," I say quickly. As though offering an excuse, I add, "You said in your book what town he lived in. There aren't that many psychoanalysts there."

"I'm not the same woman those people knew, Del," she says. "I changed my name because I am not the same person. Talking to those people couldn't tell you anything about me." I consider this as we continue in silence. "I'm not upset with you, Del," announces Virginia. "You were doing a thorough job. I have to admire that. And," she adds, "everything happens for a reason. Your actions caused me to have a very difficult and strange week. But every experience is an arrow pointing down the road of selfhood." Her saying my name so frequently makes me nervous. I feel like a naughty child, trapped and guilty, and finally grateful to be let off the hook with a scolding. I remember my conversation with Virginia's daughter, Agnes. Ginny's daughter. Both Agnes and Virginia insist that Agnes's mother no longer exists; and still, I honestly find this hard to swallow.

"Your mother is alive," I told Agnes. "She wrote three books, and you're in all of them! What do you think when you read those accounts of your childhood?"

"I'm a journalist," I tell Virginia, as we turn onto Adobe Village Road, but I regret my words before I explain the supreme importance of thorough investigation. I'm not really a journalist and we both know it. In fact, we both laugh at my tone, my face turning even redder than Virginia's. "I'm sorry," I say, though I'm not sure if this is true.

"Don't be. Don't ever be sorry." She takes off the sunglasses as I look over at her, and I see her pupils shrink to black dots. "Regret," she intones, "is the surest way to imprison yourself in the past."

We get back to the resort a few hours before the workshop's set to start, and I spend the interim lounging by the bright blue, lagoon-shaped pool with a fruity drink and some magazines. I scan the articles and flip through glossy photos of women who look as sleek and bright and sexy as Virginia Morgan, only younger. I think back to my conversation with Agnes, how I told her she and her sister should talk to their mother at least once, just to get some answers. I don't know what came over me, what made me feel I had a right to interfere in these people's lives. I even told Agnes the date and location of Virginia's Toronto workshop. "I don't really know if that would be the best thing for my sister," she said.

The workshop at the resort itself turns out to be smaller and less flashy than I expected. The audience is made up of ten women, ranging in age, as far as I can guess, from early thirties to late sixties. There is also one forty-something man. We are seated around a large conference table in a sleek-looking room with a view of the golf course. Virginia enters once we've all been seated for about five minutes. She clicks to the head of the table in her high heels and smiles, seeming to make eye contact with everyone during her five minute introduction. She finally looks like the woman in her author photos. Her hair is sleek and shiny; her makeup is smooth and, unlike the day before, doesn't look overdone. Her sunburn is merely a healthy, pink glow, and she's changed into a tailored brown suit that shows off her raw-vegetable-fed body. Although undeniably soap-star-esque, she exudes confidence and composure. "Relax," she says. "This won't hurt much." A few people chuckle; others merely smile. "You know that feeling of pulling off an old, crusty scab?" Almost everyone laughs. "That's the kind of satisfaction we're going to feel today."

As we entered into the room, we each dropped our buried burden in the labelled metal bin, and now Virginia wheels it in front of the window. She looks around for a volunteer, but no one comes forward. Catching my eye, she raises her eyebrows, and I stand up. She sprays a generous amount of lighter fluid into the metal container and smiles at her audience. "You should probably do this outside," she cautions. "I can't be held responsible for burned-down houses." The ten women and one man laugh, eyeing the bin warily. "You want to run up here and save these relics, don't you?" says Virginia, grinning. More nervous laughter. She hands me the matchbox and I lean over to see the edge of my kitty journal, now dotted with kerosene. I light a match. Virginia nods encouragingly. "Bombs away," she says. The flames spread fast, then burn high and blue, the metal can and its contents looking like a giant flaming sambuca. "Forget it!" she exclaims, and her audience joins in tentatively. "Forget it!" she yells, and I yell along with the others, "Forget it!" It's truly freeing, forgetting about that kitty journal, knowing I'll never miss it. I almost have the urge to do the same with all my old boxes of clothes and papers, like I know Virginia does every year on the anniversary of her head injury.

I look at Virginia and she's in her own world for the briefest moment, watching the fire. I remember how she warns, in her second book, against getting attached to people. Even Missy Vanderos, Virginia's agent, housemate, and closest friend, calls Virginia a loner. The two women, only weeks apart in age, met in the hospital after Virginia's fall down the stairs; Ms. Vanderos was also recovering from head trauma, in her case incurred during a car accident. Ms. Vanderos described to me how, a year after they met, she invited her new friend to spend a month at her summer house in Spain. The two have worked and lived together ever since. "But she really needs her space," the former lawyer explained to me. "She's very claustro-phobic when it comes to emotional dependencies. She really lives that stuff she writes – she won't do anything out of obliga-tion." Perhaps it's Virginia's fierce independence that makes her so appealing; I realize, odd as it seems, that I've become attached to her already, hoping we'll stay in touch and be good friends. She catches my eye and smiles briefly before motioning for me to sit back down. I'll never hear from her again.

I imagine how she must've headed out early that morning, down past the manicured palm trees and right out onto the highway. How she walked and walked for hours, not thinking of turning back, not anxious over where she'd end up, or how she'd get there. Not worrying about her growing thirst or the steadily rising sun scorching her skin. She didn't seem surprised, or even relieved, to see me. And I think of how she stopped in the middle of the narrow, wooden staircase on our way out of the Tex Mex Annex, and stood stock still in front of me until I finally said, "What are we waiting for?" I only clued in afterwards that I was quoting the quotation in her book. "It's nothing," said Virginia, tossing her hair over her shoulder to flash that disarming smile. She lifted her arms a bit like a kid imitating an airplane, and ran the rest of the way down, fluorescent thongs flip-flopping in a chaotic rhythm against the wooden stairs.

# DANA MILLS

## STEAMING FOR GODTHAB

We've been outside for months now. We're getting the way we do after so long without sight of land or a woman. Last night Vince licked my neck. It was on the way to the showers. "Come here," he said. Then he brought me in for a whisper. "Listen to what old Skipper told me." When I got close he licked me. I laughed and gave him a quick hickey on his shoulder. Really it was more like a bite though.

Vince's tales have been getting stranger. Especially over the last few weeks. No one listens to them any more. Yesterday he was going on about his granddad again. Vince's granddad said if you split a crow's tongue apart it'll talk like a parrot. So Vince tried it. Only the tongue kept slipping and rolling out of the bird's mouth. The only reason we remember that one is because him and Euclid got in quite a scuffle afterwards. About whether crows really do have tongues or not.

Two weeks on the boat you've still got fresh memories of home. You're feeling okay. You've got your morals. At least some. And your head's not completely filled with fish innards yet. Two weeks in you're still doing all right. Two months in you're not doing all right. That's when you're broke up. Being broke up is like cabin fever times a thousand in a house that won't sit still. It's being trapped in a world of sixteen on and four offs and little to no sleep. It's when things get "small and dark" like Euclid says.

The Captain gets broke up too. He's been outside so long he never came back. He likes to take stuff from us and each time it's something different. This time when we boarded we were searched for calendars and bank books and anything with a date on it. He told us we'd get it back when we dock. If Euclid is right and the Captain does have some kind of collection going then we'll never see our stuff again. "You know as well as I do that he didn't give it back the last four times out," Euclid said the other day as we put shrimp to boil, "so why would he now? Why do you think he's got a gun to guard our pile of stuff? So other people won't take it?"

The other day we brought in the net. Only there was nothing. Not even the net. I was below in the processing room sending the last shrimps down into the hold. Euclid came running in waving his big arms and head around. "They hauled back and nothing left but doors!" He was happy as anything. When they pull in the main warp and there's nothing left but the doors we chain them back and steam for land. That's all. The Captain has no other choice. He's got this hundred-by-two-hundred-foot net lying on the bottom with the cod end probably packed with a couple tons of perfectly good eating. And he's just got to leave it.

Dropping the net's never happened to me before this time but you'd always hear about other ships losing theirs. I heard foreign trawlermen talking about it the last time we docked in Godthab. I guess it's not unpopular for Japanese captains to do themselves in after something as traumatic as that. They can't face the companies. No wonder though. The companies are never happy. Especially about dropping a net. Nets aren't cheap. I imagine the Captain isn't sleeping too good right now knowing what he has to face.

Us boys doing the hauling and processing don't care too much about dropping a net though. Every one of us hopes to God we never see each other again after we get off the boat. "See you," we say when we're getting in our cars and meeting our wives and kids at the yard. "I hope I never see your fucking face again." That's how much we care about being out on the water dragging up nets. Being out here slicing. Packing. The list goes on. It's a living. That's it.

Vince tells me how his granddad had this imaginary friend. The friend had an imaginary dog. They both lived with Vince's granddad before he died. In the wintertime his grand-dad'd pretty well melt the snowbanks when he left the door open to call the stubborn mutt inside. When Vince went to see him on his deathbed he shooed Vince out. "I need my friends," his granddad said. "Can't you see them standing there waiting for you to leave?" Those were his granddad's last words. "He conked out before I could even leave the room," Vince says. "It was as eerie as hell being left alone with those two."

I wish Euclid was here in the galley. Him and Vince'd be at each other's throats. Euclid questions every story Vince ever tells. It's because he's sick and tired of them more than anyone else. "Your granddad was a horrible person," he likes to say.

"Just like someone else I know. Tell a story worse than that and I'll give you my cut of the catch."

"How's the steak?" Vince asks me. Last week we hauled back and there was this giant halibut in the end. Normally we throw anything that's not shrimp back but Vince called it the moment he saw it. "Mine!" he said. "That sucker's mine." When he strung it up it was taller than us. About four feet wide with eyes like baseballs. I don't know why he called it. He lets anyone cut a piece off and fry it. That's just Vince though. This is our fifth time out together and I'd say when he gets broke up he's about as right in the mind as his grandfather was.

"I said how's the steak I said." Vince eyes my fork as I move it to my mouth.

"Beautiful."

"Biggest one I ever caught."

Then someone shouts. "Land!" We hear it again. "Land!" But it sounds a lot like guys from up above just messing with us. We're an easy target. You can't see anything when you're eating in the galley because it's down below and the Captain's boarded up the porthole. So you've got to be careful not to get carried away. Since the haulback last week I'd say I've heard it at least once a day.

Everyone's quiet. Not even a plate or fork banging in the kitchen. You can hear the footsteps overhead.

"What did they say?" Smithy asks.

"They're saying shut your mouth," Vince says to him. "Coal miner's daughter."

Smithy stands up. All sweaty and crazy-looking. His eyes blank like a shark's. He rolls up his sleeves and holds his fork up like he's going to put it through Vince's eye. Smithy's a force to be reckoned with. He has five older brothers and was raised as a miner. "Hold still," he says to Vince. "I'm going to put this through your eye."

But he can't do it. Because when he goes to jam the utensil in he's knocked down by a big shake from the boat. Land. All hell breaks loose. Guys drop what they're eating. The cook doesn't even bother shutting the freezer. Land. It does this to people and you'd never know it unless you spent months away and were double broke up.

Vince got a couple sheets of tickets from the Captain. Since we're in Greenland we're going to need them. Tickets can save you from waiting in line outside the bar. You can also have a bunch of girls around you by the end of the night. Tickets are what allow you to buy drinks. Plain and simple. If you don't have a ticket you can't buy a beer here. It's the system to keep people from drinking their whole lives away. Since boats come in and out and a lot of guys get tickets from their captains it doesn't always work too good though.

"Vince. Let me buy some tickets."

"Talk to the Captain. He don't care about anything right now. He gave me two sheets."

I have to pass by the Captain's door to get to the back of the lineup. You can see him inside talking to guys but also eyeing our stuff. He's gotten even skinnier since he dropped the net the other day. The lineup moves pretty quick. But when I'm number two the Captain says to the guy ahead of me that that's the last sheet. I have to get right in there and ask if he can rip it in half since there's no one behind me in line. "Unh

unh buddy," the guy in front says. He's a monster. He's no threat though. He's one of the biggest guys on the ship but he can barely chain the doors back himself. "First come first serve," he says. "How about I get you a tall one at the bar. How about that?"

I want to grab him so bad. I have my moments where I'd say I'm almost triple broke up and something like this can really trigger it. "You should rip it in half," I tell him.

"No can do son."

You learn pretty quick being outside that you can't take that or they'll walk straight over you. "Look boy. Sell me half for twenty," I say. "First thing back to Novi I'll get you the money. Or I can give you kroner right now."

"I said no can do."

I give the bearded beast a huge shove. Right into the door frame. The guy moans. So the Captain bangs his bony hands on his desk. At first I think he's telling us to take it deckside. Then I realize he wants to see a fight. "Grab the tickets from him," the Captain says. So I try and grab them.

"No way," the monster says. He puts the tickets behind his back. "No fair buddy. You've got the Captain on your side."

"No fair?" I push him again. "Just give the tickets then. Rip them."

The guy takes off. So I run after him. The Captain comes out into the hall. "Grab the tickets!" he screams. "Grab his leg. Trip him!"

The monster heads downstairs. I push him into the fish jackets but he's so excited to get off the boat that he just bounces off. That's when one of his buddies comes out of his room. Daniels. Daniels is known from here to Moncton and back to be a scrapper. Daniels took Euclid out one night when Euclid put a stingray down his back.

"Just rip them in half," I tell him. "I'll buy them off you. Come on."

"Take a hike," the monster says. Then he slaps me across the jaw. But not as hard as he could since Daniels is right here. "If I see you at the bar you're dead," he says to me. Then he gives Daniels half his tickets.

Vince is alone in his quarters listening to *The White Album*. He's singing along with "Piggies." All the other guys have gone already. "How'd you do?" he asks. He's got his only set of good clothes on. "Get any tickets?" Vince sprays some cologne in the air and walks through it. I don't know why the guy bothers really. He's always reminded me of those fish that pop when they hit the surface. Those ones whose eyes and tongues get picked at when we throw them to the birds.

"I'll have to get some from you," I say. "You got two sheets didn't you?"

"Come to me at the bar and I'll give you whatever you want."

"I'll just buy them now."

"I said you don't have to buy them I said. Just come to me at the bar."

Most people in the city are wearing parkas or large jackets. All Vince and I have on are our wrinkly good shirts. This place always reminds me of Newfoundland. And it can remind some Newfies of it too. Once instead of "land" I heard a Newfie shout "home" when he saw Greenland in the distance. You've got to be pretty broke up to do that though. The land's kind of the same in places but the houses are different. More European. And you'd never see a Benz taxi and a dogsled team cross paths on the Rock.

Vince waves his sheets of tickets in the air. The bouncer nods his head for us to come forward. Some people in line aren't happy about us getting in. Either that or they want our tickets. Trawlermen tend to get more than the locals do. There's some shouting in broken English and Danish. Mostly Inuit though. The bouncer puts all his fingers in the air. So Vince rips off nine tickets.

Inside they're playing Scandinavian disco music. Flashing lights are everywhere. So are Inuit girls. They've all got these tinselly scarves on that make them seem really exotic. Almost European but not quite. Half the guys from the boat are up on the floor already dancing with some of them.

Vince rips me a ticket.

"Come on. Give me a few."

"That should do for now," he shouts in my ear. "I've got to preserve these things."

At the counter this girl who can't be even fifteen yet says something to me in Inuit. I shrug my shoulders. She tries some English. Beer and buy are the only words I get. I hold up my one ticket so she'll understand. Then a trawlerman who's on the other side of me says, "She means if you got an extra ticket she'll buy you a drink." Vince is hard to track down but I find him at the back talking to a couple girls and handing them tickets.

"Give me another ticket will you."

"I don't like how you ask," he says to me. "Didn't I just give you one?" Then he starts laughing really hard. I feel like grabbing him. He always gets cocky in front of women. And when he gets cocky he starts telling stories. "Listen hard to this," he says. He always says that when he's in his cocky place.

So Vince goes on about how his granddad had two horses that could tap dance. He used to take these horses around to the carnivals and play the flute while they did their thing. "Granddad had to go to a special blacksmith," he says. You can tell the girls don't understand any of it.

"Give me twelve." I shove a wad of kroner into Vince's hand. "Give me twelve."

Vince laughs. Then he hands the girls more tickets. "Listen hard to this," he says. Then he looks straight at me with those buggy eyes. He laughs with that mouth of his. So I push him hard into one of the speakers.

"Give me twelve," I shout in his ear, "or I'll do something you won't like at all." Vince's ugly face smiles but I know he's just testing me. I look serious enough. Serious enough that he rips me off ten.

"What were you going to do?" he shouts. All of a sudden he's a little serious too.

"Never mind," I tell him. "I just hope I never see your fucking face again."

The girl is still at the bar waiting. So I buy her a drink. She tries to give me money for the beer. I say no thanks. "Next time," I tell her. I can see she's already got a hold of some tickets tonight.

We get out on the floor. I'm taking her around all the bodies like we're ballroom dancing and she's loving it. I can tell she thinks I'm good. She's not bad herself. Her little hands are small. The beer makes them colder. Her cheeks are soft as anything. They make me wish I'd shaved so I could feel closer to them. I like to pick her up and swing her around. With all the lights behind her she's this mystical Inuit goddess who landed right in my hands.

It feels like we stay out on the dance floor for hours. It pretty well could be because I go back and buy us more beer every twenty minutes or so till my tickets are gone.

Around last call I'm swinging her in the air again. That's when her legs bump into that same monster who wouldn't give me the tickets on the boat. He pushes me and the girl over on the floor. Some dancers step on us. Our last beers pour over us but we're still laughing. She kisses me. Then the guy kicks me and my eyes go all teary. So I cover her head to make sure she's all right.

When I get up the guy is nowhere in sight. With his size he'd be easy to spot. He's long gone. So I brush myself off and tuck my shirt in. I tell her to wait. Then I go check if I've got any blood on myself. When I get back she isn't there either. I check the women's bathroom and out behind the bar but I can't find her anywhere.

I stumble past the factories and back to the water. It takes me quite a while to find our boat because a few have docked since. I can see my breath and my spit freezes before I can walk over it. All over the city there's laughing and screaming and people lying in snow and grass and mud. A lot of the girls are going to the boats.

There's this moaning when I get back on board. At first I figure it's just two people back aft. But it sounds different than that kind of moaning. So I check it out. Halfway under some rubber is my girl from the bar. Her face is covered in black marker. She's still got all her clothes on. And you can kind of tell they never did anything to her. They just let her pass out there I guess. When I pick her up she looks straight at me like I'm going to hurt her. Then she relaxes. She sees it's me. I find an unmarked spot between her black moustache and glasses and kiss it.

I take her downstairs to wash. After a while she sits up by herself on the toilet. Hand soap doesn't do much so I go down and grab some sanitizing chemicals from the processing room. One of them does a decent job. After I'm through with her face the marks are only about half as dark. But you can tell that's the best it's going to get. Just when I think I've made the situation better she starts moaning again. It seems like she might be trying to tell me her name. I give her some water. That and me scrubbing at her face wakes her up a bit and she stands up to go.

Through the galley doors to the kitchen you can see a group of girls eating out of the freezer. They laugh and throw shrimp and spit juice at each other. "Get out of there!" Euclid screams at them from the belly of the boat. "Stop that and get in here!"

We climb up on deck. That's when we meet Vince coming back. "Listen hard to this," he says and points at her markered face. The two Inuit girls he's with laugh pretty hard. Not as hard as Vince though. Vince looks like he's having real pain. Like he's so broke up he's never going to resurface. Like he's on the same wavelength as the Captain.

Soon enough Smithy boards the ship with a couple of the boys. They all start riding me like anything. They'll never let me get away with this without razzing the hell out of me.

"Where's your girls?" I say. "Or do you even swing that way?"

"What? You call that a girl?" Smithy says back. "He hasn't shaved in weeks."

You can tell she's getting scared of them. She takes my hand. Doesn't let it go. She pulls me through the streets but in a different direction than the bar. Now there's less and less screaming and fewer bodies lying around. She pulls me to these red warehouses. Huge complexes. Euclid said most of Greenland lives in them but he doesn't know anyone who's been inside.

There's a hunk of plain plywood nailed onto the wallpaper in her living room. Tape over the broken window. Which makes it not much warmer inside than out. From the height we're at you'd think there would be a view but all I can see are lights from the side of another building.

Some guy who must be her brother sits in an armchair smoking a cigar. He wears this brown yarn scarf. He says something to her in Inuit but I can't tell if he's angry or not. He sets down his cigar and comes over. His face is gold and it stares right at me.

I look down at his hand. I don't know if I should shake it. "Hello," he says as if he knew I'd be coming.

She takes me into a small room. She's drawn all over the walls in there with paint or maybe even black marker. Just wavy faces and arms and legs. On the ceiling there's posters of Hollywood stars. Her clothes are all over the floor and there's a small pile of them by the closet. There's a mattress with no sheets. Just these old blankets bunched up. The whole room has a cold smell to it like a winter bonfire.

She kisses me. I try and turn the light off but she pushes my hand away from the switch. I pull her shirt off and my eyes catch her belly. They drew fish swimming around. Some even push up out of her pants. I keep thinking it had to be that monster who wouldn't sell me his tickets. The guy who kicked me. All I can think about is the different ways I'm going to kill him.

She gets into bed with the lights still on. I follow her. "Jesus. It's freezing in here," I say to her. My teeth are chattering away. "It's colder with the blankets on." She laughs but I can tell she didn't understand much of it. She slides her hands up under my shirt. Then into my armpits to make them warm. Her nose is cold against my neck. I can't move. I'm still too furious.

When she brings her hands out they're the warmest things around. She rubs my stomach. She rubs it till I'm not angry any more. Till I've forgotten about being broke up in that boat with them. Till I've decided I'm staying in Greenland. If not forever then at least till after they've left for Nova Scotia.

# THÉODORA ARMSTRONG

## WHALE STORIES

The scratching of the pine needles on the roof woke William from a dream that left his armpits damp. The wind crawled through the trees, weighing down the boughs, forming fierce patterns on the wall above his bed. An empty pillowcase tacked above the window frame by two push-pins covered the bedroom window. His mom hadn't found time to buy curtains yet. They didn't have a kitchen table or a TV or a couch or a doormat. The bed and breakfast was bigger than their house in the city, and for now most of their furniture went into the guest rooms.

There was something else – another noise, some sort of animal snuffling and pawing at the side of the house. Shaking himself out of his covers, William flipped on the bedside lamp and checked the alarm clock. It was already nine-thirty. He pushed the pillowcase aside and opened the window an inch. The wind cried through the crack, spitting salty air into his face. There was a clatter of garbage cans below and he caught sight of a scruffy tail disappearing under the porch: one of the wild dogs again.

At the end of the yard, the huge arms of the pines rolled like they were trapped in an underwater storm. The clouds collected in giant dark barrels along the mountainside. He could see a small section of the beach through the thick cover of pine trees, the waves reaching up, breaking and then dropping onto the grey sand. William yanked the window shut, rattling his rock collection that sat in a tidy line on his windowsill. The rocks came from Australia, Africa, South America. His father was a geologist and travelled all over the world collecting samples from the different continents. The travertine rock – his favourite – fell to the floor, careening under the bed, but he had no time to find it this morning. He dressed quickly, pulling on his dark blue sweatpants and a grey hoodie. He had planned to be up hours earlier, before his mom and his sister, but he hadn't slept well last night. He kept hearing footsteps and voices in the upstairs bedrooms. He still wasn't used to the B&B, the strangers in the house moving around at all hours. The floors were rough and creaky, and it took him a while to figure out how to sneak around soundlessly. When the guests left for their daily outings, he would open the doors to their rooms – something that his mother warned him not to do. He only ever took two and a half steps into the room, and from that point craned his neck to get a look inside their suitcases.

In the mornings, William's mom left their breakfast on the kitchen counter or in the oven to keep warm while she bounced back and forth from the dining room, serving the guests. Her cheeks were always pink and she smiled widely with only a small crinkle of concentration on her forehead. She did look happier to William, but only when she was working, cleaning up, or listing the best spots to go kayaking. The guests came from Ohio, or Toronto, or Oslo. Instead of opening their home to one traveller – his dad – his mother now opened it to all of them. William sometimes felt like one of his own rocks, but much bigger, rooted in the middle of the ocean, with people from interesting places drifting past on their way to somewhere better. His mom kept saying this was her dream, something she never could have done if she was still with William's father, living in the city.

In the kitchen, his younger sister, Miriam, sat on a chair, her plate of waffles balanced on her delicate knees, the plate looking dangerously unstable each time she cut herself a small bite. William could tell Miriam had already spent most of the morning outside. The knees of her jeans were grass-stained and she was wearing her red rain hat. This was probably her second breakfast.

"Where you going?" she said.

William grabbed a waffle from the counter and ate it standing up. "To the beach."

"It's going to rain."

William shrugged.

"You don't have to go to the beach every day you know. I found a hollow tree. Just past the road up there," she said, motioning behind her with her fork.

"Good for you," William said, stuffing the rest of the waffle in his mouth.

"I can show you where it is."

William ignored her, gave her a half-hearted wave goodbye and headed outside, grabbing his pocket knife before shutting the kitchen door. He kept it hidden in his rain boots by the coat hanger. His father had given him the Swiss Army knife last year on his ninth birthday. It had come all the way from New Zealand in a large, yellow manila envelope with his name written in big capital letters across the front. His mom and dad had fought about it over the phone, about whether it was an appropriate gift for a boy his age.

The wind tugged at William's wet hair and crept up the sleeves of his hoodie, sending a shiver down his back. He took the porch steps two at a time and bounded for the forest. The trees swayed back and forth, their bare spiky tips slicing through the dense fog billowing off the ocean. Usually it took him a while to cover the distance between his house and the beach, because he often stopped to watch a beetle's progress or to unravel the tight coil of a worm with his finger. But this morning he hurried along the path, anxious to get to the beach. William scowled as he hurtled past one of the B&Bers standing in the backyard – a birdwatcher with expensive-looking binoculars. He couldn't understand why his mother loved to share their space with these strangers. Back in the city, they had a large fenced-off yard where there were never any birdwatchers getting in his way or little kids wanting to play little kid games or kayakers flapping around in the water like angry birds. Whenever there were children staying at the B&B, his mother always coaxed him and his sister into playing with them. Miriam seemed to enjoy the other children, drawing them into her make-believe games where she was often chasing them, pretending to be an elephant or a rhinoceros. She, in fact, seemed lonely and sad when the children were gone. William, however, preferred to be alone. Too often the children were much younger or had no interest in rocks or traps.

First thing to do this morning was to sharpen a stick. He wasn't sure why, but he had a feeling. The wind had knocked down lots of branches, so it wasn't hard to find a good one. He positioned himself on a rock, the branch laid across his legs, and whittled the wood to a sharp point. A ragged dog, its grey coat matted with dirt and burrs, ambled over and William stiffened as the dog sniffed at his stick and his feet. He was wearing sandals and the dog gave his bare toes a lick before trotting toward the beach.

The dogs were a problem in the area. His mom said it was probably cottagers bringing their pets on holiday with them. Maybe the pets ran away or the owners were cruel and didn't want them anymore, but the dogs were left behind. They bred and there was a pack of them now, all mutts, dogs turned wild. He never touched them. Many of them had sores or bits of their ears missing. Their eyes were shifty and they panted even when they weren't running. Usually they left people alone and you'd only see them when they went rummaging through the garbage cans. At night it was hard to tell them apart from the coyotes. William was sure he heard them sometimes, following him through the woods, or watching him while he was on the beach. Some of the other residents would shoot the more troublesome ones, but no one really felt good about that. There was always a lot of talk in town about what to do about "those damned dogs." Everyone called them "those damned dogs." Even his mother and she never swore.

The second thing William had to do this morning was to check the hole. He walked up the beach toward the rocky outcrop to the west, whacking at the tall ferns that grew on the outskirts of the sand with his new spear. The waves had left deep tidal pools along the rocks and he splashed through them, scattering tiny fish and sending crabs scuttling to their hiding spots. He loved the sound of their legs scratching across the boulders. On any other morning he would have stopped to peer into the puddles, maybe sent Miriam for an empty ice cream bucket so they could collect specimens. Miriam was meticulous about it, counting each crab, noting the ones missing legs or with odd markings, and giving each one a name. But this morning he was in a hurry. He wanted to get to the hole as quickly as possible.

He had done this every morning since they moved to the Sunshine Coast. It had taken him a long time to dig the hole. And it had taken him a while to pick a good spot. He chose an area protected by a rocky outcrop that stretched right into the ocean and hid the beach from view. He dug a couple of small trial holes and decided on a spot near the treeline where the sand was still damp, but where the hole wouldn't fill with too much water. The first week he started digging right after lunch and only stopped when it was dark and he could hear his mother's voice yelling "bedtime." He had worked straight through the noon heat, taking breaks every fifteen minutes and running into the ocean to splash water on himself. In ten minutes he'd be dry again, and by the end of the day his body had grown a second salty skin. The first week had been hard work.

The second week it rained, and he was down in the hole every day with a bucket trying to keep it from caving in. He found an old abandoned shed back in the forest. It was covered in moss and half the roof had sunk in. The windows were thick with spiderwebs. He pulled some old boards from the siding, dragged them through the forest, and propped them up along the sides of the hole, trying to hold up the walls. Luckily, since then, there'd been a dry spell.

In the third week, with the weather hot and sunny again, the hole was deep enough that it provided a little bit of shade while he worked. The challenge in the third week had been getting in and out of the hole. One day he had dug so fast and deep that he couldn't get back out. For a while he had been convinced that he had captured himself. He screamed for ten minutes straight and no one came. Then he sat and cried for another five. He imagined Miriam peering down at him with all her questions and then going to tattle, or worse, the B&B kids wandering over and staring with their googly eyes. They would think he was some sort of treasure or a wild sea creature, wet and thrashing, trying to get back to the water. Finally, he discovered that he could claw his way out, but that meant partially refilling the hole.

The next day he rigged a long rope that he found in the abandoned shed to a nearby tree and used that to get in and out. The rope was dry and brittle, but it held. When the hole was deep enough – almost two feet taller than William – he covered it with large branches. He warned his sister not to go to that part of the beach. He told her there was a dead whale with its eyes pecked out, and that it stank so bad you would throw up on the spot if you went anywhere near it. She kept away from that part of the beach, but every few days she would ask him if the whale was still there. He would tell her about the whale in different stages of decomposition: the tail munched away, the fin all droopy and slimy, crabs happily eating away his huge whale tongue. Miriam would listen to his whale stories and wrinkle her nose. Sometimes she'd gag or pretend to plug her ears. One day, he guessed, the whale would disappear and he wouldn't have to lie anymore.

He never worried about his mom wandering to that part of the beach. She liked to walk east, probably because it wasn't so rocky. The beach stretched out smooth and glossy at low tide, as if the land and water were one. William's mother warned them to be careful walking out on the sand. The ocean could be tricky, could sneak around you until you were left standing on an island alone. Miriam had become paranoid about this and kept one eye trained on the ocean at all times when she was beachcombing. Their mother's walks were a habit now and came after dinner without any announcement. Miriam and William were never invited along and knew not to ask. For the first few evening walks, Miriam would clutch the porch railing and cry, believing their mother was never coming back. But now they barely blinked as she quietly escaped the house. William still followed her though, but always at a distance, watching her from the forest. He would crouch behind the tall ferns, his breath shallow and painful in his chest. She stopped at a different spot every time, and when she found her spot, she would sit on the beach and sink her hands deeper and deeper into the sand, staring out at the water. Sometimes she sat for a couple of minutes and sometimes she sat for an hour. The longer she sat at the beach, the greater the chance she would cry. When she was finished, she stood up and wiped off her bottom, but with her hands covered in sand, she usually just made it worse. There was always sand in the house. She made William and Miriam take off their sandals and hose off their feet before they came in, but for whatever reason, she didn't notice when she tracked the sand in herself.

For the past two weeks, William had been waiting and hoping. He hoped that at least something small would fall into his hole, and if he was lucky something bigger. He wondered about the hole at night when he was in bed. Sometimes the wind tricked him and he thought he heard a yelp or crying. On those nights he hardly slept, waiting for morning to come so he could go check out his catch. But there was never anything in the hole. A couple of nights earlier, he had an idea that came from watching one of the B&Bers fishing one day, something important he hadn't thought about before: the hole needed bait. While no one was watching, he slipped the rest of his bits of beef from his dinner plate into the pocket of his shorts, and while his mom took her walk, ran to throw them on the branches covering the hole. Before he threw them on he had pulled out his pocket knife and cut them into smaller bits, just in case it was a very small animal that came along. He'd done this every night for the past three nights: chicken, fish, and last night, pork.

William had dug a hole once before when he was much younger. Actually, it was his father who had done most of the digging, with a small, yellow plastic shovel that came with the beach set his mother had bought for him. They had gone to Spanish Banks for the day. His mother was very pregnant with his sister and lounged on the beach blanket that his father set up in the shade under a tree. William spent the entire day running back and forth between his parents at top speed, helping his father with the digging and pressing his ear up to his mother's belly. His dad kept saying, "We must be on our way to China."

Back then, William couldn't understand why they had never gotten there. That night his dad had to explain that China was very far away and that it would take years of digging to get there, that it was much quicker to fly or take a boat. But William was disappointed. He felt misled. Looking at the speckled rocks half buried in the sand, he tried to remember where his father was right now. Digging somewhere in New Brunswick, he guessed. He was fairly sure that was the last place. When they moved, they left all of his father's clothes and books. His mom said it was easier for their father's work if he left his things in the city.

"Hi," a small boy said.

William had been planning his attack if he found something in the hole and almost walked right into a kid. The kid was definitely one of the B&B guests and a couple of years younger than William – young enough that his parents still dressed him. William could tell by the way the boy's shirt was tucked in and cinched with a miniature belt. His hair was carefully combed to the right side of his forehead. He was standing in gumboots ankle deep in a tidal pool, pushing around a large bit of Styrofoam with his foot.

"Where are you going?" the boy asked.

William was surprised by the question at first, but realized he must have been walking with purpose. "None of your business."

"Can I come?" the boy asked, looking hopeful.

"No." They stared at each other blankly.

"I made a boat. It was for the crabs to float on. But I can't find any," the boy said, motioning to the large piece of Styrofoam.

"Doesn't look like much fun."

"Nah, it's not really. You want to help me sink it?"

William didn't bother answering. He raised his stick and whacked the boat, sending bits of Styrofoam flying everywhere.

"Wait for me," the boy yelled, running to the beach. "I need a stick, too."

William paused mid-strike and waited for the boy to return with his stick. The two boys swung and swung until all they were hitting was water, and tiny Styrofoam islands floated all around them.

"It never sinks," the boy said.

"Nope." William brushed bits of Styrofoam out of his hair. "I gotta go."

"Where are you going?"

"I told you already. It's none of your business." William started back on his course toward the rocks. The boy followed behind him for a ways, and when the boy didn't turn back William swung around to face him. "I said don't follow me." The boy took a couple more steps and William realized that maybe the boy was older than he thought, just small for his age. William raised his stick. "Don't follow me or I'll stab your neck."

From the top of the rocky outcrop William had a good vantage point. He could see the boy walking back to the B&B – probably to tell on him. And he could see the hole. Something was different from the day before. The branches had shifted slightly, but he could tell they had definitely been moved. The meat was gone. Maybe the wind had moved the branches or a bird had tried to pick up the meat. Or maybe something had fallen in. He scrambled down the rock and ran toward the hole, sliding into a crouching position right at its edge. As he leaned over, he accidentally kicked some sand into the hole. A faint shuffle and a sigh escaped from the depths of the trap. He sat back a moment and thought about the sound, listening for something else. His entire body shook with expectation and fear. His hole had trapped something; he didn't know what to think. In his hurry he had dropped his stick behind him. He ran back to grab it and crouched down again, taking some deep breaths. Slowly, with his eyes squinted in anticipation, he began to pull the branches away gently, one by one, setting them down in the sand behind him.

The creature at the bottom of the hole was shadowy, but he could still make it out: a dog. A small one, maybe a year old. It was grubby, a mutt like all the others; its brown and gold coat was spotted with bits of rough skin from too much scratching. But it was still alive and that wasn't what was supposed to happen. The dog was lying in a few inches of murky water. The ocean had seeped into the hole over the past week, bit by bit. The sand William had kicked in was scattered across the dog's belly and on its face. The other dogs were hiding somewhere else – dozing under porch decks or cars, sniffing around the forest, eating garbage. But this dog couldn't move. Its front legs seemed to be bent back too far. It was blinking, trying to get the sand out of its eyes. When he had imagined the creature in the hole, it was always dead. Most of the time it was a skeleton with bleached white bones and he took the skull home and put it on the steps of the porch. Other times it was a bit messier and he had to do real man's work. The knife came out on these occasions but the thing was always partly decomposed. It was never a broken thing. And it was never a crying dog. The dog had started to whimper and give little yelps. William walked the circumference of the hole and came to the conclusion that the dog was dying. He turned from it and ran.

Back over the rocks he slipped and fell and didn't feel a thing, didn't even check his knees for gashes. He could still hear the dog's whimpers. He ran across the length of the beach and up the path to the B&B. He ran through the empty living room and into the dining room. There was a family sitting at the dining-room table: a mother, a father, two girls, and the boy from the beach. They stared at him in stunned silence. The boy grimaced at him. William's mother was laying out one of her many maps of the area.

"What have you done?" she gasped. Her face crumbled, and William was sure his mother already knew everything.

"I'm sorry, I'm sorry," William choked, out of breath from running.

"Oh, your knee. What a mess, come here. Let me have a look."

William had forgotten his knee. He looked down. Bits of gravel were embedded in the pink flesh and the blood had spilled over the torn skin and trickled down his leg. It made him ill to look at his own blood and the tissue under his skin.

His mother pulled him into the kitchen, away from the guests' prying eyes. She picked him up and sat him on a stool, ran a clean cloth under the tap, and pressed it to his knee. She carefully cleaned around the edges and patted the raw centre, gently picking out pebbles with a small pair of tweezers. "Always into things." She frowned, trying to look stern. She rinsed out the cloth and ran it up and down his leg, wiping off the blood. The cloth was cool. It felt wonderful to him. He wanted to take it for the dog.

"What happened?" she asked.

William shook his head. "I slipped on some rocks," he whispered.

"Well, you have to be more careful." His mother inspected his knee once more. "I never get to do this anymore. You're getting too big," she said, grabbing a large Band-Aid from one of the cupboards. She sealed up the cut, grabbed his shoulders, and then patted his cheek. "Be more careful next time," she said. "Why don't you play inside now."

William wanted to take a nap but he couldn't sleep. He remembered his rock and slithered under the bed on his stomach. He carefully placed the travertine back between the whale-shaped sandstone and the almond-sized quartzite. He ran his hand along the windowsill, gently brushing the rocks with the tips of his fingers, watching them spin slowly. He had placed the quartzite in his mouth once and chipped one of his molars. The travertine was his favourite though, smoother than the other ones and ringed in rusty reds and ambers. His father had given him the rocks as presents – not all at once, but one at a time, so his collection had grown slowly.

Whenever he returned from one of his trips, his father would pull a new rock from his shirt pocket. Sometimes he would give William a rock right in the middle of the airport, with William still wrapped around his neck in a hug. Other times, William had to wait until they reached the parking lot, aware the entire time of the hard lump pressed to his chest, as his father carried him to the car. And sometimes his father forgot all about the rock. The next morning there would be a stone sharing William's pillow. He could see his father's long fingers with their carefully clipped nails – he kept them very short to keep the dirt from collecting under them – turning the rocks gently as though they were as fragile as eggs. He would smooth his fingers over their surfaces, giving them a particular sheen. Over time they dulled and William would rub them furiously with his own fingertips without any results.

Miriam never got rocks as presents from their father. She got notebooks, or fancy pencils, and once she got a large shell full of the sounds of the ocean. Later, their father explained that the shell did not contain the sounds of the ocean, but rather the sounds of the inner workings of their ears – their blood and bones.

William opened the window and stuck his nose outside. The wind had let up and the clouds hung low and full. A stillness had fallen over the beach, the occasional lap of a wave the only sound, no longer rhythmic, but stuttering and sad. William knew he had to go back, but he didn't feel like hurrying anymore.

When William reached the hole, the dog had stopped crying. It was lying quietly, taking in shallow breaths. Another, older dog had come and lay near the hole, his tongue hanging out sleepily, his spotted belly exposed. William kicked sand on the old dog and it raised its head a moment, before letting it drop back with a thump. He yelled at it and hit it with his stick.

"Get out of here, mutt. Stupid shithead mutt, move."

The dog rolled over onto his back, panting heavily up at William, his paws swimming in the air. He kicked more sand on the dog. He kicked sand everywhere: at the old dog, at the dying dog. The dog in the hole started to whimper again and then yelp, short piercing cries that bounced across the water. William sat down and pushed at the sand with his feet and hands. It only took him an hour to fill the hole. Much less time than it had taken to dig.

As William climbed back up the rocks, a light sprinkling of mist coated his face and arms. By the time he got to the top it started to rain, fat silly drops that hit him in the eyes and trickled down his forehead in streams. When he touched his face, he could feel the red heat of his cheeks. The wetness in his underarms was the same as in the morning. He stopped at the edge of the rocks to take a few deep breaths. He could see Miriam in her red rain hat trudging up the bank toward the house. He turned and watched the rain patter over the mound where the hole used to be. He watched the drops smooth the surface until that part of the beach looked exactly like every other part of the beach. He stayed on the edge of the rocks until his jeans were soaked and the flush had drained from his cheeks.

When he got back to the house, Miriam was sitting on the floor in the living room braiding a strange blond girl's hair. The girl sat poised, one knee bent, as though she was ready to bolt instantly, but Miriam still had a firm hold on one of her braids. The other stuck out crookedly from the back of the girl's head. It looked painfully tight. The bang from the kitchen door woke his mother, who was napping on the couch beside the two girls.

"Is the whale still there, William?" Miriam said, without looking at him. She was still focused on the blond girl's hair.

"The whale?" he said, confused for a moment.

"Yeah, the dead one. I saw you by the rocks."

"No," he said. "No, it disappeared."

"What whale?" his mom said, sitting up now on the couch. The left side of her face was lined with sleep creases.

"There was a huge whale down that way on the beach with no eyes. The birds ate its eyes," Miriam said. She finished the braid and the little girl instantly stood and ran into the dining room without saying goodbye.

"A dead whale? Why didn't you tell me about this?" His mom looked worried.

"William said it was a secret. He said if you smelled the whale, you'd barf."

"William, where on the beach was it?"

"I don't remember."

"Past those rocks," Miriam said. William bent down and pretended to be busy taking off his shoes. He picked at the knots in his laces.

"Well, I hope you didn't touch it. William, take those sandy shoes outside." His mother sank back down onto the couch and curled up like she was getting ready to go back to sleep. "How could it just disappear?" she said through a deep yawn.

William pulled off his shoes and looked at his hands. He had sand under his fingernails. "It doesn't matter," he said. "It's gone now."

# MIKE CHRISTIE

## GOODBYE PORKPIE HAT

### PURPOSE

I'm lying on a bare mattress in my room watching a moth bludgeon itself on my naked light bulb. Over near the window sits a small television I never watch; beside it, a hot plate I never use. I spend most of my time here, thinking about rock cocaine, not thinking about rock cocaine, performing rudimentary experiments, smoking rolled tobacco rescued from public ashtrays, trying to remember what my mind used to feel like, and, of course, studying my science book.

I dumpstered it two years ago and ever since it has lived beside my mattress like a friend at a slumber party, pretending to sleep, dying for consultation. I read it for at least two hours every day; I know this because I time myself. It's a grade ten textbook, a newer edition, complete with glossy diagrams and photos of famous scientists looking so regal and concentrated, the flashbulb having caught them mid-paradigm-shifting

93

thought. I like to think that when they gazed pensively up at the stars and pondered the fate of future generations, they were actually thinking of me.

I excavated the book in June. The kid who threw it out thought he would never have to see science again, that September would never come. What an idiot; I used to believe that.

My room is about the size of a jail cell. One time, two guys came through my open window and beat me with a pipe until I could no longer flinch and stole my former TV and a can of butts, so I hired a professional security company called Apex to install bars on my window. I spent my entire welfare cheque on them, just sat and safely starved for a whole month. I had to pay the guy cash upfront because he didn't believe I could possibly have that kind of money. It felt good to pay him that kind of money; he did a good job.

Someone is yelling at someone outside, so I go to the window and look out into Oppenheimer Park, which sits across the street from my rooming house. There I see only a man calmly sitting on a bench. Everyone says this park was named after the scientist who invented the nuclear bomb. It has playground equipment, but it's always empty because no parent would ever bring their kid there, on account of it being normally frequented by people like me or Steve or worse. The park is infamous, an open-air drug market they say. From my window, I've seen people get stabbed there, but not all the time. Good things happen in the park too. Some people lie in the grass all day and read. The people who are reading don't get stabbed. I'm not sure why that is.

The next day, I cut across the northeast corner of the park and walk east up Powell. I approach a group of about six Vietnamese men. You can always tell the drug dealers because they're the ones with bikes. I purchase a ten rock with a ten-dollar bill, all of my money until Wednesday. I stare at the ground while one of them barks at me. He is cartoonish, his teeth brown, haphazard tusks. Frowning on eye contact – somehow it seems to make things more illegal – they all shift side to side on their toes like warmed-up boxers and aim nervous glances at the street. "Pipe?" they bark. No, I say, I have one thanks.

Crack melts at a tepid eighty, and if you heat it too fast, it just burns off with minimal smoke. Smoking it is one thing I'm good at. I don't really feel the crack craving people talk about; I would describe it more as a healthy interest than anything else, like I'm fine-tuning a hypothesis, or conducting a sort of protracted experiment. I know it sounds strange, but I feel if I could get high enough, one time, I would quit, content with the knowledge of the actual crack high, the genuine article. Unfortunately, a paltry approximation is the only high I have been able to afford so far.

In an alley, my brain has a family reunion with some long-lost neurochemicals, and I crouch beneath the party, not wanting to disturb it, shivering and euphoric next to a dumpster. A seemingly infinite and profound series of connections and theories swamp my mind. It is a better than expected stone and it makes me long for my room and my book.

A man and woman are five feet away, arguing. I am unsure how long they've been there. I have an urge to explain something complex and scientific to them, to light their eyes with wonder. The man is talking. "Hey bro."

"Hi are you guys doing okay?" I sputter, feeling sweat rim my eyelids.

"Oh yeah, she's just being a harsh bitch . . ." He turns and yells the last word in her face, actually puffing her bangs back with it. After an emphatic pause, he turns back. "Hey bro, how about you give us a toke and make us feel better?" he says to my clutching hands with a smile and an assumed entitlement. I'm briefly embarrassed for being so absurdly high and unable to share it with them or anyone else.

I tell him, "It's all gone. Sorry," with what I feel is a genuine sincerity, my high already beginning it's diminuendo.

"How about giving me my pipe back then?" he says, steps closer.

I've been on the receiving end of this type of tactic before. I tell him sorry, there is only one, careful not to combine the words *my* and *pipe* – a pairing that would no doubt signal the commencement of my probably already inevitable beating.

The woman tells him to leave me alone. Her cropped shirt reveals a stretch-marked abdomen harbouring unearthly wrinkles the texture of a scrotum or an elderly elephant. The man is yelling now. Blurry and ill-advised jail tattoos populate his arms and I watch them wave above my head. I wonder if any woman who has told her boyfriend to leave somebody alone has ever meant it. If ever, I conclude, it is a statistically insignificant proportion. Amidst his racket, the urge to smoke another rock comes over me in a bland revelation, like I need to do the dishes. I hear rats scrabbling in the dumpster and I try to think if I have ever seen a rat look up, into the sky I mean, and wonder if it is possible for them to see that far. As I'm trying to stand, the man kicks me in the chest with his fungal shoe and I feel a crunch inside my shoulder and it begins to buzz, and I bring my other arm up to shield my face.

I heard my pipe hit the ground, but it didn't break because crack pipes are made of Pyrex, the same glass as test tubes. People dumpster them from medical supply laboratories. They are test tubes with no bottom, no end, all that smoke and mania just funnels through them unhindered. My lungs have tested the tubes and their acrid samples, but unfortunately there has been no control group, so the results of these experiments are often difficult to observe.

I am crumpling to the ground, hearing him pick up my pipe and smelling the tang of fermented piss under the dumpster. When urine evaporates it leaves a sticky yellow film, and I am thinking about how urine is a solution, not a mixture. Of this, I am absolutely sure, and the beating continues from there.

### MATERIALS

In the room beside me lives an old junkie named Steve, who at some indeterminate point took to fixing between his toes, the rest of his veins being too thickened and prone to abscesses. He blows his welfare cheques in about three days, pupils whittled down, head pitched on the stormy sea of his neck like an Alzheimer's patient. He warns me by banging on the wall when he suspects he may be about to shoot too much dope. I've rescued him twice by calling in the Narcan injection, plucking the needle from his foot before they arrive with their strange antidote. I guess you could say he is my only friend. Steve knows nothing of science. Doomed to forever repeat the same experiment, he arrives on his sticky floor at the same vomit-soaked conclusion over and over. I'm well aware that experimental replication is a cornerstone of the scientific method, but not to the extent Steve takes it.

In his nasal junkie voice, he calls me tweaker or a coconut because I smoke crack, but it doesn't bother me. He doesn't actually mean anything bad by it. One time he sold me a kernel of soap, saying it was a rock he found on the street and would let go for cheap. At first I didn't believe him, but it was the way he held it, with reverence, two hands together, a child holding a cricket. I didn't speak to him for weeks until he almost over-dosed, and when he woke up, he'd completely forgotten ripping me off, so I forgave him, plus I stole the money back anyway. And I guess I was lonely.

Steve has been bringing me food. He says he might as well, because the guy on the other side of his room doesn't do shit when he bangs on the wall. Tins of grey meat you open with a key, and day-old hamburger buns from the gospel mission. My left collarbone is broken and my face raw and taut with swell-ing. Bones float and snarl in my shoulder like an aluminum boat running aground, and there have been inexplicable dizzy spells. Last week, I stumbled to the welfare office, picked up my cheque, saw my worker, Brenda #103, and told her every-thing was okay while she made her empathy face and told me I should go to the clinic. "I should," I said, and staggered to the cheque-cashing place, returning home with a small fortune in Tylenol 3s and a tin of tobacco. The T-3s came from a guy I know who long ago convinced a doctor of his unbearable chronic pain, resulting in a bond I suspect is not dissimilar to love. I gave Steve some 3s for taking care of me and he took them all right away, hand to his open mouth, in a yawn.

It's a month later, I've been up for days trying to memorize the periodic table and I'm so high my stomach is boiling. I sold the T-3s and bought some crack because I've found that it's what best alleviates the pain and the dizziness, but now the crack is all gone and the reckless similarities between magnesium and manganese are beginning to make me want to dig my teeth out of my head like weeds. I'm watching my light bulb grow brighter, grinding my molars, and wishing I had someone to apologize to. I guess it's ironic that only when I'm really stoned do I feel optimistic and strong enough to never want to do it again. I'm telling myself that when I get my next cheque I'm going to get a big bag of weed and some groceries and just get healthy again.

It's morning, my room is a haze, I still haven't slept, and I'm lying face down in bed listening to the inside-my-head sound of eyelashes crunching into the pillow. It reminds me of distant steps in snow. I'm fluttering them faster and faster, imagining someone running toward me, their breath steaming into the air, and suddenly I hear my fire escape rattle.

I snap into a sitting position and there is a man at my window. He wears an old-style porkpie hat and a three-piece tweed suit, and is smoking a tailor-made cigarette that smells American. He grips the bars of my window as if he has been momentarily locked up for a petty misunderstanding and smiles warmly.

"Hello Henry, my name is J. Robert Oppenheimer."

The man's speech is soft and melodic. His eyes are soothing and blue, lit by an inquisitive intensity. I recognize him from my science book.

"I recognize you from my science book," I say, my teeth chalky and soft from grinding.

"Of course Henry, and dare I say I recognize you as a fellow of the pursuit? Would you agree? And by pursuit I'm referring to the intrepid and arduous quest for knowledge, am I correct? Care for a cigarette?" His eyes linger on my science book as I tentatively snatch a smoke through the bars, not sure which of us I would describe as being inside.

I find my hands are shaking as I light the smoke. I'm not used to tailor-mades and get panicked by the filter's restriction as I wait for the drag in asthmatic anticipation. I exhale and begin to calm. His eyes flash as he speaks.

"I feel it's the best way for a man to buckle into some erudition, just a meagre room, a book and some tobacco . . ." He is taking strangely long drags from his cigarette, and as he exhales, his eyes scan the room and land on the vials that once held my crack supply.

"I'm sorry Mr. Oppenheimer but . . ."

"Call me J. Robert, what my students call me."

"I'm sorry J. Robert, I mean thank you . . . but I'm pretty sure there are two dates under your picture in my textbook or rather what I mean to say is that . . ."

"I'm deceased? Throat cancer, unequivocally abhorrent, avoid it at all costs, only truly evil things expand infinitely my friend." He grabs the bars and gingerly sticks his long, spindly legs through, then his arms, assuming the position I imagine would be most comfortable were one trapped in a giant bird-cage. I can see his socks and they don't match.

"What're you doing here J. Robert, if you don't mind me asking?" I mumble as he grips my eyes with his, brandishing the smile of a forgiving and benevolent parent. There is silence, he is still smiling and staring; I'm not sure if he heard me. He seems to be thinking.

He smacks his thin lips and lifts his palms upward and out in a gesture of peace as his long arms sweep farther into the room than I ever imagined they could. "Look, I'm not concerned with the past. I can see by the shape of your face and shoulder you are not particularly interested in revisiting it either. I'm here to elucidate, provide guidance, this sort of thing, do you have any questions so far?"

My mind accelerates with a myriad of science-related questions, questions I've never had the chance to say out loud, and all of them seem too elementary for his finely tuned understanding. "Did you know the park out there is named after you?" I sputter, my clamping jaw carving jagged chunks out of my syllables.

"Ha. Of course it's not, Henry. It's named after Vancouver's ghastly and colitic imp of a second mayor, David Oppenheimer – no relation. Why would they name it after me?" He lights up his third cigarette in one mechanical motion and blows more smoke into my room.

"Everybody around here thinks it is," I say.

"Regardless, your question is churlish and time is precious, so moving on, I will cut to it . . ." He clears his throat. "In my humble opinion it is not possible to be a scientist unless you think it is of the highest value to share your knowledge, would you agree?"

"Yes," I say, still wondering if churlish is bad.

J. Robert's eyes again find my empty crack vials. "And accepting this axiom you must agree as a scientist that it is invariably good to learn, that knowledge is good? Yes?"

I nod.

"Do you truly believe that?"

"Of course," I say, sounding decisive and intelligent.

"Excellent. So now we arrive at the crux of my proposal, Henry, and that crux being . . . In the spirit of scholarly inquiry, I hereby formally request your assistance in the procurement and consumption of the drug commonly referred to as crack cocaine."

"I have no money," is the first thing I can think of. The next is wishing to have denied ever smoking it.

"Ahah! A pragmatist! Of course I have more than adequate funds to suffice for our purposes, think of it as our research grant, and when I say *our*, Henry, I am illuminating the fact that you will be an equal participant in the inhalation of the psychoactive substance in question."

I say nothing. His eyes are so kind and forgiving, they make me want to turn around and see if they are actually meant for someone behind me.

### METHOD

Although he is too foreign-seeming and well-dressed to be a cop, J. Robert's eagerness and complex questions put the dealers off. However, even when turning him down, they treat him with more respect than they ever did me, calling him Sir, one of them going as far as to ask why such a fine gentleman wants to get high with a goof like me. Finally, after promising to report all details of the experience, I convince J. Robert to stay back while I complete a transaction. The man is impressed by my large request and American money and says he is from Seattle and is just selling to get home. He stuffs J. Robert's money into his jeans before telling us he has to go pick up more vials because he doesn't have that much on him. I follow him nervously with J. Robert trailing a block behind. He leads us to a rooming house and I wait for a minute while he runs upstairs. I don't have to find out what J. Robert would do to me if I got burned for his money because the man returns with a plastic bag rattling with vials, and I act like the whole thing was no big deal.

The sun is out and fluffy clouds bump together in the sky above the park. Clouds are glorified smoke. My days are defined and determined by the comings and goings of various types of smoke. We are walking briskly, J. Robert slightly ahead of me. We come upon an old drunk woman who lies at the edge of the park, passed out before she could reach its boundaries, pickled in the sour jar of her body. I get a whiff of mouthwash vapour, strangely sweet and ironically fresh. Her mouth is loose and open, jaw pushed slightly forward, like she is concentrating on something fragile and complicated. "Alcohol evaporates faster than water," I say, and J. Robert is too far ahead to hear me. It's as if this woman is sublimating, I think, solid straight to gas, her life's horrid memories fuming from her rubbery ears. I tighten my grip on the bag of vials and quicken my pace.

"Your apartment is significantly smaller from the inside, Henry," he says as he flips through my science book. He tosses his suit jacket over my TV, unbuttons his sleeves and shoves them up his arms. This is the longest I have ever gone between buying rock and smoking it. He rubs his hands together, sits cross-legged on my mattress. "Teach me everything," he says. "Everything you know."

As I'm laying out our supplies: pipes, brillo, lighters, mouthpieces, it starts to rain. It feels as if the room's air is being sucked through the bars, out the window and up into the churning clouds, and I feel cold. I explain the entire process to J. Robert, savouring the details, making it sound as complicated as possible. He studies my face while sometimes moving his lips along with me as I talk.

He raises the pipe and his hands are shaking.

"Like I said now, don't scorch it."

I can't believe I'm telling a genius to be careful. He does a good job melting it and starts to get a toke, but he lowers the pipe trying to watch the rock burn and the liquefied crack dribbles out the end into his lap.

"Goddamn it!" he says with an intense and boyish concentration.

I start coaching, "Don't stop! Keep smoking it, tip it up, that's it, now inhale – go go go go . . ."

He brings it back to his lips frantically, musters a pretty good one, but blows it out too early. "I don't feel anything Henry, goddamn it, show me properly you buffoon!"

"Here," I say, blowing on the scorched pipe to cool it down. I load another rock, cook it, take a big hoot, then hold it to his lips and he fills his lungs. He holds it, blows it out and shivers.

His porkpie hat is tipped back like a newspaperman and his forehead is glossy.

"That was the one Hank . . . Oh yes . . . I'm getting the picture." He closes his eyes and leans back on my bed. "I'm experiencing the prologue of an extremely pleasurable sensation now, differing vastly from what I imagined however, but quite promising."

I help him smoke more rocks and he is chain-smoking cigarettes, pacing the limited circumference of my room.

"It's no secret I'm a vastly superior theoretician than experimentalist, this is a reality I have always accepted." I can't imagine how deeply he is thinking.

"Oh Hank, without your steady hand, your know-how, I would be a stranger to these marvellous sensations. I feel such a marked increase in self-control, vigorous and capable of productive work."

"I'm glad I could help," I say.

He kneels beside me. "Henceforth, I shall refer to you as Hank Aaron, because, Hank, I propose you just keep on doing what you do best, hitting those little delectable balls out of the park for me? Hey, old man? We can be partners. What do you say?"

"Okay," I say, "partners," gazing into the horde of vials, hearing the rain ticking in the trees.

Either he or I wants to smoke another. So we smoke another. He begins a series of brisk push-ups in the centre of my room.

"Christ, a man with your kind of prowess Hank, we could've really used you at Los Alamos, just imagine it, the world's greatest intellects, working together in seclusion, a truly cooperative effort to stop the greatest evil mankind has ever known, nature's deepest secrets unfurling before us like the desert mesas."

J. Robert is grunting with exertion and the rain is making the trees outside tell him to *sssshshhhhh*.

He finishes, which serves as a good reason to smoke more.

"We could've had a building erected specifically for ingestion; this substance would have tripled both creativity and productivity instantly. A sizeable supply could have been requisitioned, and of course rationed and distributed equally. Oh, we would have had a functional device years earlier, we could have vaporized Berlin as soon as Hitler jumped a border for Christ's sake. Hank, I once tired of your platitudes, now I see you for who you are, a great probing and unflinching mind, steadfast and brilliant in the greatest of fashions, but yet modestly so, not a snivelling blowhard of pseudo-academic tripe, but a scientist, in the most unmitigated sense of the word."

I can't believe what he is saying. My throat burns and I feel like I'm going to cry. I stand up and start telling him about some experiments I've been performing and start moving my hands dramatically like he does as I talk, and I'm explaining about how I have always felt I was born in the wrong time in history and about if I just maybe had a chance to meet some peers or like he said some fellow scientists with similar interests and now that he is here . . . there is a bang on the wall. It's Steve.

Robert comes with me. We are companions. Steve's door is open and we find him nodding out on his bed with his legs splayed in front of his frail body, semi-conscious, his head drifting downward toward his feet. I shake him and he comes around.

Steve says something about his high being ruined. Robert

introduces himself and immediately offers Steve some crack, offending him deeply.

"I don't smoke that shit Bob, it don't do nothing for me and as far as I can tell the sorry people who really like it, I mean the people who really get it in their blood, are the ones who already hate themselves the most."

His eyes are still rolling back in his head, and he is speaking completely through his nose as if it were a kazoo. "That's why I shoot dope, because I'm selfish, because I treasure myself. And I just don't mind that self, the one I care about so damn much, feeling like it's floating in a warm sea of warm tongues every single minute for the rest of its life, that's all. Is it so awful Bob? My advice is you leave my crackerjack friend here out of your . . ."

Robert's voice booms theatrically, "Sir, I must ask you to hold your tongue! Love yourself? How asinine! It's philistines like you who cloud the great minds of our nations with your rhetoric of self-worship. This crack cocaine unleashes the truest and noblest potentials in our society! And furthermore . . ." but he trails off because Steve has nodded off again, and this time I don't wake him up, just glad he knows so little of science as to not recognize J. Robert and rat him out. Rat him out to whom I'm not sure.

Back in my room, J. Robert's fuming anger is now transforming into a sort of agitated sadness. I think it is probably also due to the fact that he is starting to come down, but I don't tell him. He comments on the naked futility of existence, the mercilessness of my light bulb, and then says something in what I think is Dutch. The rain has stopped. Luckily, he wants to smoke more rock, which is good because I do too.

"What made you want to smoke crack in the first place?" I say.

"Excellent question. Because Hank, to have a sound and crystallized view on something, I feel one must experience it first-hand, to know what one is talking about that is, and this crack just seems like an area I should form an opinion on."

I notice sweat stains forming in the armpits of his crisp white Oxford shirt. I want desperately to pick up where we left off, before we were interrupted, eager for him to listen to some more of my theories.

"You know, J. Robert, these pipes are made of Pyrex, the same glass as test tubes."

"Simple physics, ordinary glass would shatter if subjected to this type of treatment, just like us, huh Hank? Steeled by the girders of inquiry and knowledge!" He shakes my shoulder and it stabs with pain, but I don't tell him to stop.

But the scientific conversation doesn't last. Robert is pacing and anxious; he wants to go outside, see the sights, meet the locals, get some air, and, of course, buy more crack. He has loosened his tie. I fear J. Robert will forget about me if we leave, or that he will disappear and never come back. I tell him we have more than enough to last us the night, and that this neighbourhood is ugly and dangerous and unscientific and we should just stay here and just smoke and talk. He snatches his hat and coat, begins stuffing his pockets with vials, and speaks: "Hank, my colleagues call me Oppie. And Oppie is not going to tell you what to do, but Oppie and his narcotics are going outside, into this night – this night whose force shall break, blow, burn, and make us new!"

## RESULTS

I was twenty-six when I first smoked crack. Crack. It sounds so ridiculous even when I say it now, so pornographic. I started late in relation to most. I'd just moved to Vancouver, just like everybody else. I was at a party I'd overheard some people talking about that afternoon at a coffee shop. Right when I got there, a girl I didn't know asked me if she could borrow some money. I asked her what for but she wouldn't say. I told her whatever it was, I would like to be in on it. I was drunk; I didn't think I would have sex with her, but I guess I hoped.

After the first glorious toke, I calmly asked how much of it was hers, how much of it was mine, took my share and left. I fumbled through the dimly lit rooms of the party and out the door, secretly deciding to smoke rock forever.

It's still forever and we are wandering the streets at the mercy of Oppie's random fancies. Often breaking spontaneously into a run, he is oblivious to traffic or fatigue. I give chase and am barely successful in my effort to stay with him. When I do catch up, he puts his arm on my shoulder, breathing heavily. He seems surprised to see me and tells me he's glad I'm here.

The pavement is wet and reptilian, the air thick with evaporation. People are out tonight, like every night, hustling, smoking, chatting, screaming, and shaking hands. Everybody is buying, selling, or collecting things of certain or possible value. Oppie is smiling and saying hello to random people and handing out cigarettes and American change to any and all who ask.

Faces drift into our orbit and out again like comets, trajectories forever altered by Oppie's generous crack policies and philosophical musings. He is electric and alive. His interest is insatiable. Lecturing as he walks, he relates mind-bending scientific concepts with ease and grace. We are a team. Although nobody recognizes him, I feel proud to be partying with such a distinguished man of science. Prostitutes approach him and he respectfully tells them he has no interest in "erotic labour," but gives them rocks and kind words. He is a gentleman.

Sitting on a bench in Pigeon Park, we form an accidental alliance with a Native kid whose face, crusted with glue, is making sad and sluggish approximations at consciousness. Oppie is offering him the pipe, but I don't think he even sees it. Oppie blows out a hoot and continues with a conversation I wasn't sure we were having.

"Take this young man for example, Hank. Here is a fellow theoretician, a physicist; he studies zero as we consider infinity. He's asking the same question we do, but he's approaching it from the bottom up, beginning with base assumptions, attempting to divide everything by zero. And as you well know, it is at these extremes, in these margins, at these points curves avoid like poison gas, that things really get interesting!"

"I think he is just trying kill himself Oppie, you can call it whatever you want I guess."

"Oh no, not kill." With wild eyes he is scratching under his shirt collar. "Destroy, Hank, he seeks to destroy himself."

When we leave, I turn and see that the kid has managed to stagger after us for a few blocks. But he can't keep up.

Oppie ducks into a corner store to buy more cigarettes. I'm straining to remember what it was Oppie actually did as a scientist. I know he made the bomb, but I'm not sure why or when. I can only remember his picture.

I decide to ask him when he returns. "Oppie, when you were working at the place in the desert with all the other scientists, all working together like you talked about, did you imagine making a better life for people in the future? I mean, did you wonder about how things would be for them?" He spins and grabs me by the neck of my T-shirt. His hands are weak and the cherry of his cigarette dances millimetres from my face.

"I want you to listen to me very intently you smug son of a bitch. In our minds, the Krauts could have dropped one on us at any time, understand? We never had any idea what was going to be done with it, is that clear?!?" I lie and say it is.

It is later, and we are on the bus because Oppie wanted to "experience the authentic transport of the proletariat."

The bus seems to cheer him up, so I ask him where he lives and he says he's been sleeping between the stacks at the university library. I ask him how a genius can die of smoking-related throat cancer and whether he knew it was bad for him, and he tells me to stop tormenting him. I want to ask him what it's like to be dead, but I don't want to push it.

"Hank, I feel crack cocaine may affect you in a profoundly more negative fashion than it does me," he says, a little snidely. "I believe it has permanently altered your judgment."

Sometimes I do worry about things like lasting damage, tracks laid down that can never be picked up, that sort of thing. I often try to remember what it was like to not know what the crack high feels like, and I can't. In this way crack rewrote my history. I remember my mother, who quit smoking cigarettes when she had me and said she dreamed of them almost every night until the day she died. Even when we ate chocolate-chip cookies in bed while watching TV, she would tap the cookie with her index finger after each bite, ashing the crumbs carefully into a little pile on her plate.

"Don't worry about me. Just hope it doesn't run out," I say to Oppie, hoping it won't run out.

A woman with a baby is sitting across from us and I wonder why the baby is up this late. Oppie plays peek-a-boo with it for a few blocks by hiding his face behind his hat. Then Oppie lights a smoke, takes a big drag and blows it right in the baby's face, and chuckles as the woman freaks and we get kicked off the bus.

Back on the sidewalk, I notice Oppie's smile has become strained and his face bleached. He now insists on carrying all the vials himself, and he has recently begun to mutter. His walk has warped into an exaggerated parody of someone trying to walk with confidence. I wonder if he is a ghost and whether ghosts get the same high. I try to imagine what is going on inside his brain. What an instrument to be flooded with so much cocaine, in this city, at this time! Just to think of all the money it would take to construct and map the synapses of such a brain. His mind is like a Ferrari errantly entered in a demolition derby. He mutters something about the "allure of alkaloids" and then something about someone named Prometheus and a vulture and a rock. "You want more rock?" I say, and he nods like a little boy. I need to keep him away from people for a while.

We run out of rock shortly thereafter, and I try to convince him we should slow down. Oppie pulls out his roll of bills like the cavalry and hands the whole thing over to a man whose face I will never remember.

"I think this new batch of stones may be cut with something vile, Hank," he says later, glancing at me suspiciously. When I shut my eyes there is a dioramic theatre of brilliant neon, and I have resolved to keep them open so as not to lose Oppie if he starts to run.

We've ducked into a doorway shielded from the street by a tile staircase. In a further effort to slow him down, I suggest maybe Oppie should try to cook up a rock on his own for once.

"Well that certainly contravenes the terms of our agreement Hank, now doesn't it? I supply the goddamn rock, you, the steady hand and experimental know-how! Isn't that it?" He is starting to yell again, so I don't press the issue. We smoke more and I hold the pipe. I'm saving the better hoots for myself because he doesn't really need them, and because he is starting to annoy me. He starts kicking the bus shelter in front of us with his leather shoe, over and over, trying to break the glass, laughing insanely. When I tell him the shelters are made of plexiglass now, he says he already knows that, although he doesn't stop.

We find ourselves back in the park that isn't named after him and I'm beginning to worry that Oppie is losing his mind. Occasional forays into madness are, from what I understand, pretty standard issue for a genius, but this seems to be of an assortment darker and more potentially irreversible. He is incoherent, mumbling in a heinous amalgamation of many languages. His teeth are yellowing and his fingers are blackened from gripping the charred pipe.

Aside from the playground, a few trees and a brick structure lie on the perimeter of the park, but mostly it's just a field.

Oppie is rocking back and forth, staring into its dark centre. I'm thinking about whether or not this is the highest I've ever been and conclude statistically it must be, but somehow I feel clear and alert. Could there be an upper limit? A cap-like terminal velocity or super-saturated solutions? I figure we need more data. I can see my room from here, and although I want to go home and read my book, and although I know there is probably already enough resin in my pipe to keep me high until at least tomorrow, I resolve to stand by him, to ride it out, that is if it can be ridden. He needs me.

He hasn't said anything for about an hour when my brilliant thoughts are interrupted by his voice, raw from smoking and disuse. "By the mere existence of this city, would it be safe for me to assume the Cold War went all right Hank?"

"Yeah, it went okay Oppie."

"Oh good," he says, momentarily clearing his throat. "That's good."

### DISCUSSION

At the skid-row country and western karaoke bar, it's me, Oppie, and the woman who told her boyfriend not to break my collarbone, our beer glasses hydroplaning around a small, slick table. She is wearing Oppie's porkpie hat in the way some women flirtatiously grab and wear men's hats, perching it on top of her hair like she is balancing it there, her neck stiffened, hoping the novelty of it will promote a new appreciation of what's beneath.

She is smoking too many of Oppie's cigarettes, and I want to tell him she broke my collarbone and watch him rise to my defence, reducing her to tears with a bombardment of scathing quips. I decide against it. She and the beer seem to be providing Oppie with some kind of deranged ballast, amnesty from the psychotic twister in his mind.

Earlier, after we'd left the park, Oppie unexpectedly scampered into a dense patch of traffic, disappearing until I found him a few blocks over with this woman on his arm. This place was her idea. Oppie had introduced me as "Professor Hank." I scoffed when he said it, annoyed by how proud it still made me feel.

The two karaoke microphones have been monopolized by an old, drunken couple who have feuded, proclaimed, wept, reconciled, and so far barely made it through a single song without regressing to bouts of screaming "I fucken love you!" alternately into each other's faces. Somebody said the guy who runs the karaoke show got bottled a few hours ago and walked home.

I'm in the bathroom now, hoping Oppie will be there at the table when I get back. Everything, even the ceiling, is wet. The urinal is old, a stainless steel trough. I'm pissing and it sounds like a sink. This is the kind of place where the line between beer and piss is blurry and rusted out, the substances confused and indiscriminate, where one seemingly unifying golden liquid soaks everything, spewing and spilling from spouts and cups.

With my steaming face in the dirty mirror, I come to the grim conclusion that I have to smoke more rock or I have to go home, and I consider stealing the stash and making off but it seems too fiendish, and plus I think he could find me anywhere.

I return to the table, where his arm is around her and she is talking: "They named that piece-of-shit park after you huh? If you ask me sweetie there shouldn't be a public square inch in this neighbourhood."

Oppie is smiling and vacant. He carefully finishes his beer and rises weakly from his chair. She turns to me and asks if she has seen me before and I say no. Oppie mounts the stage and the old couple unexpectedly surrender the microphones to him. He brings them both to his mouth at the same time and begins.

"Good evening ladies and gentlemen, my name is J. Robert Oppenheimer and I'd like to thank you for this opportunity to speak before you this evening. I want to commence by buying everyone in the house a beverage as a sign of my esteem and gratitude."

No one cheers because no one is listening. A synthesized slide guitar strikes up the next song.

"No takers? Good, because I'm all out of money, which means there are only a few ivory nuggets left between me and something dark and unknowable."

Oppie clears his throat. Someone yells something in the crowd, but it's not directed at him.

"Crack cocaine ladies and gentlemen, some believe only the truly unhappy enjoy it, or rather need it. However, this hypothesis seems flawed. I have found its benefits extremely promising, but sadly, not without cost. Like most things it is a good servant but a bad master. Thus I believe control to be paramount, wisdom and knowledge trumping blind fear and temperance. To speak of regret is to ignore realities and inevitabilities. Humanity, my friends, must experiment, that is its nature. Want versus need, nature versus nurture, these questions seem redundant, boorish. Knowledge cannot be outlawed. It must be doggedly pursued! Alas, eggs are broken, unfortunate experiences are experienced, but, however, in my opinion, humanity is stronger for it."

No one is listening. Without his hat, in the awful stage light, Oppie sways feebly. His hair is grey and sparse; his cheeks, hollow and triangular. He looks so different now from my science book photo. He is pacing the stage, compulsively touching and scratching his face as he speaks. He looks like one of this neighbourhood's regular, discarded men, who in a dirty and ill-fitting tweed suit is taking an unscheduled narcotic vacation from the drudgery of his blister-packaged medication.

"And so, I stand before you, yet I am dead of throat cancer as my colleague pointed out so perceptively earlier this evening. How is this possible? Who can say. What is possible is that if I go to sleep, I suspect I will never wake up."

I wish he had a podium, something to put his hands on.

"Therefore, I must conclude, further study is merited. And I must forge on, like Currie with radioactivity humming in her oblivious cells, with courage, conviction, and a deep, unshatterable hope and faith in the value of this experiment. And for this undeserved opportunity, I humbly thank you."

The woman, still wearing his hat, stands, clapping proudly. When he gets back I ask him if he wants to leave, to go back to my room and just talk science and smoke cigarettes. He says I haven't heard a word he's said all night.

## CONCLUSION

We are in the parking lot next to the bar.

On the street, the car is waiting. A piece of paper taped to the back window indicates it is insured only for today, and it billows grey smoke as it idles. I know her boyfriend is in there too, but I don't look in because it doesn't matter. Oppie is leaving.

"We are going to go and appropriate a few computers from the university library and sell them in an effort to procure some powder cocaine that Brenda here is going to cook and formulate into some real pure samples, genuine freebase, no more vials and uncontrolled specimens," Oppie says as I load our last rock. I want to tell him to stay, but I am too tired and confused and plus I don't really want him to.

He does not ask me to come with him and I do not want to go. I'm worried I will regret it. I've never smoked real free-base. Someone else will be helping him now and they will probably do a better job than me.

I hold the pipe to Oppie's lips a final time; he exhales and his voice is a scoured whisper. "Well that's the last of it, Hank. You truly are one of the finest minds of your generation. How I'm going to miss your steady hands and gentle flame."

He is really tweaking now, his eyes drifting inquisitively to pebbles on the pavement, his shoulders and arms moving restlessly like he is trying to get rid of something disgusting riding on his back. As if he is trying to shed his body entirely.

The car is honking in the street and I'm going to cry. "These people are not scientists Oppie."

"No, but they can help me, they know things my boy."

"Were you serious about worrying you'd never wake up?"

"I guess so Hank. I'm not sure. Crack may not be the panacea, but I enjoy it like nothing I've ever experienced. I refuse to stop. Not now, not when I feel like I'm so close to a breakthrough."

"I'm sorry I didn't take better care of you."

"Nonsense, I planned for all this to happen."

He touches my shoulder, it twinges painfully, and he says, "To be frank, I think the world in which I shall live in from now on will be a pretty restless and tormented place; I do not think that there will be much of a compromise possible for me between being of it, and being not of it."

I watch him get into the car and he is gone again.

# SCOTT RANDALL

## THE GIFTED CLASS

On the last day of school, when Vice Principal Garner visited the classroom right after the nine-thirty bell, the students knew she would probably come many times throughout the day. Mr. Ryan pulled the door shut behind him after the two of them stepped out into the hall, but their voices could still be heard in the classroom. All of the doors in Wellington Elementary were raised an inch off the floor – in case there was a fire, according to Billy Pace – and whenever Vice Principal Garner visited, the entire grade two gifted class fell quiet so they could listen in.

"He said it'd depend on next year's budget."

"And when will that be announced?"

"Late July usually. Sometimes into August."

"Eleanor, I'll be back in grad classes throughout the summer."

"I know."

Closest to the door, the students seated at the Green Table heard the conversation best. Belman Oz, Billy Pace, and

Marla Rosebush stopped working on their morning project –
cutting cereal boxes and toilet rolls and reassembling the cardboard pieces into three-dimensional geometric shapes – and
the only sound in the room was the squeaking of the gerbils'
exercise wheel.

Marla leaned closer to Belman and whispered.

"Eleanor."

She raised her eyebrows, and Belman nodded.

Some of the students at the Blue Table and Orange Table
resumed taping together their pyramids and rhombi, but the
room was still quiet when Mr. Ryan re-entered. He smiled and
said Mr. Nasaga and Mrs. Agana sure were getting a good
cardio workout this morning.

Mr. Nasaga and Mrs. Agana were the class's pets, but
Mr. Ryan preferred to call them the class's subjects, two brown
gerbils who lived in an aquarium lined with wood chips and
covered by a wire-mesh screen on top. Belman turned to look
at the animals and saw Mr. Nasaga digging excitedly into a
glass corner and Mrs. Agana running on the steel exercise
wheel. Or maybe Mr. Nasaga was running and Mrs. Agana
was digging; it was sometimes hard to tell them apart.

Above the aquarium, Mr. Ryan had posted three computer
printout banners on bristol board. *Do not pick up Mr. Nasaga
and Mrs. Agana without Mr. Ryan's supervision. Do not feed
Mr. Nasaga and Mrs. Agana snacks from home. Mr. Nasaga and
Mrs. Agana are anagrams of anagrams.* One of the banners was
almost too faint to read because it was printed on a dot-matrix
printer, and the letters in the other two were streaked with
small white lines. Those banners came from the bubble-jet
printer. The school had bought two new PCs for the gifted class

when Mr. Ryan started in September, but he was still waiting on the money for new printers.

Drifting from table to table, Mr. Ryan repeated *good work*, *nice job*, and *grand*. That was a word he used a lot. *Grand*. The tables weren't really tables, but three desks pushed together into triangles for group work. While Mr. Ryan was still talking to the Red Table, Billy Pace raised his hand and waved it until Marla told him he had to wait his turn.

"Sorry," Billy said. "My mother says I sometimes will get impatient because Dr. Fitzgerald switched me from Ritalin to Dexedrine and my body needs time to adjust."

Billy had changed medications five months earlier, just after the Christmas break, but he continued to mention it regularly. He said the Ritalin was effective, but his mother and Dr. Fitzgerald made the decision to switch him to Dexedrine because Ritalin was too conversational.

"Controversial," Marla corrected him.

"Yeah, that too."

Belman thought Marla was the smartest student in the class. And she was sweet too. When his dad moved out of the house two months ago and Mr. Ryan announced that everyone had to be extra conscientious around Belman, Marla was the only one who treated him the same as before. Her parents lived together, she explained, but they had never actually married, so maybe matrimony wasn't so important as everyone thought.

Her geometric shape was a cone that she'd made by cutting a toilet paper roll down the side and twisting the brown cardboard.

"Good work," Mr. Ryan said. "Sometimes the most clever ideas are the most simple ones."

"Belman's is just a square," Billy said.

"It's called a cube, Billy, and I believe it also looks quite grand."

Ever since his parents split up, Belman noticed Mr. Ryan had grown less serious about Belman's work. At parent-teacher night in January, there had even been talk of moving him into a destreamed class for the third grade, but that subject seemed to have disappeared. Now Mr. Ryan asked him how he was doing almost every morning, and said that if Belman ever wanted to talk, he would listen.

"I guess a cube is all right," Billy said.

The next subject of the morning was math, and so the students all lifted the tops of their desks to remove their abacuses. The lesson was fractions, and Belman tried hard to follow along. Whenever he found he couldn't, Marla would whisper to him and pivot her abacus in his direction. Billy spent most of the lesson flicking the wooden beads along their metal rods – just to watch them bounce back – but whenever Mr. Ryan called on him, he came out with the correct answer.

"Twelve-fifteenths," he said.

"That is correct."

Billy waved his hand.

"Which can be reduced to four-fifths. Or zero point eight zero."

————

At first recess, the gifted students were allowed to go out in the schoolyard, but most of the class chose to stay indoors. The older grades tended to hog the swings and slide no matter who got there first. And besides, recess was when Vice

Principal Garner would probably come back to see Mr. Ryan again, and no one wanted to miss that.

Belman took his morning snack from his bookbag and was disappointed to see that it was once again a Fruit Roll-Up. Grape. He unrolled the purple sheet on the top of his desk and slowly lifted the cellophane film from one corner. Shapes of a car, bus, train, and truck were moulded into the sheet of pressed fruit, and he studied them all before offering Marla a bus.

"Or you can have a train if you want," he added.

"Thank you, Belman."

She placed a round shortbread on his desk.

"Did you know Fruit Roll-Ups have gelatine in them?" Billy asked. "And gelatine comes from horse's and cow's feet? Ground up into a powder that is finer than salt but not as fine as talcum powder. Probably from sheep and goats also. My parents won't buy them."

Belman nodded and chewed on a car.

"Jell-O too." Billy said. "But not pudding."

Billy had told him this before. Last year, they were in the same class, a split senior kindergarten/grade one gifted class. Teachers like to seat students alphabetically, and so Belman imagined that he would probably be sitting beside Billy Pace until at least junior high. One of their projects in grade one had been to construct a mobile, and Belman had hung four stuffed fish from his wire hanger. They were only paper fish, but he'd folded his paper before cutting so he could have two identical fish silhouettes, and then he'd taped along the outsides and stuffed them with crumbled Kleenex tissues. He'd even drawn blue and green scales on each fish.

Billy now mentioned the mobile whenever Belman was

unable to produce a correct answer and whenever he took longer than everyone else to finish a project.

Belman's other Green Table partner, Marla, had transferred to Wellington, so she hadn't been in the same gifted senior kindergarten/grade one class. On the first day in September, when Belman met Marla, Mr. Ryan asked everyone to stand up for introductions, and she told the class that she was originally from Chicago, which was in the state of Illinois in the United States of America. Her mother was a lawyer and her father was a professor of French and Spanish, and they moved to Toronto, Ontario, Canada, because he was offered a new job. During her introduction, Belman thought he should tell her that his dad was a professor too, but he taught classical studies instead of French and Spanish, and he worked at a community college and not a university, which Belman's mom said was not like being a real professor at all.

When the students had finished their first-day speeches, Mr. Ryan announced that he wanted his turn, and stood up. His first name, he said, was Alex, and his middle name was Trevor, after his grandfather. He was a vegetarian, which meant he didn't eat animals, and his favourite food was spaghetti. When he was in elementary school, he explained, he was put into a gifted programme as well, and the experience had changed his life. It was grand. He wasn't married and he had no children, but one day he wanted them. Then he was quiet for a bit, and he added that he hoped his children would be as clever as everyone in his new class.

The students had clapped.

With their snacks finished and the wrappers put into the garbage where they belonged, Marla asked Belman if he wanted to go look out the window with her. He knew she wanted to ask about his mother's new boyfriend. She wanted to know whether or not the man had spent the night over at Belman's house yet. The new boyfriend's name was Frank and he was a fireman, a job that held a lot of influence in the second grade. Except for Marla, Belman hadn't told anyone about him.

The side window was lined with Dixie cups holding the class's bean sprouts. Each cup was labelled with masking tape, on which the students wrote their names in red and green Magic Marker. Belman's bean sprout hadn't risen out of the dirt yet, but there were other cups like that, so he didn't feel bad about it.

Marla leaned against the window ledge, and Belman told her that Frank the fireman still hadn't stayed over yet.

"Well," she said, "they've only been together a month."

"He has to work a lot of nights." His mother had told him this. "So they only see each other Fridays and Saturdays usually. Sometimes Sundays."

Marla assured him that Frank the fireman would sleep over soon.

"You'll be watching TV on a Saturday and he'll come downstairs and say good morning to you."

Belman couldn't imagine it.

"He'll still look sleepy and your mom will be all distracted and faraway when she makes your breakfast."

They were quiet for a moment and then Belman said firemen make good money.

"Better than community college teachers, my mom says."

Belman nodded, and then Marla asked if he thought

Mr. Nasaga and Mrs. Agana were a couple or just two gerbils who shared an aquarium.

The ten-forty-five bell rang and all of the gifted second graders returned to their seats. Mr. Ryan was still out in the hall with Vice Principal Garner, but he turned around and looked through the door window when he heard the bell.

He came back into the room smiling.

"Good news."

He waited until he was at the front of the class by the Purple Table to explain.

"We will be getting new printers for both computer work-stations in about a week. One of them will be a colour printer too, so we can print out images and photographs we find on the Internet."

Billy raised his hand and waved it.

"What photographs?"

"Oh, I don't know, whatever we need for history or science or current events."

Billy waved his hand again.

"We'll be in grade three, so really only you and your next-year students will get to use the new printers."

Mr. Ryan was still smiling, and he asked the class to take out their *New Horizons* readers and turn to page twenty-eight. Everyone should try to read the story by him- or herself, he said, but when they were done, he wanted the tables to answer the comprehension questions as a group.

"Uncle Leonard" was about a boy who inherited his uncle's stamp collection after his mother's brother died suddenly. Belman wondered how the man died, but the detail wasn't something the author included. Most of the story was about how the boy – his name was Jack Pierre – organized all of the old stamps into an album. First, Jack wanted to arrange the stamps by how much they were worth, but it turned out they were all from different places with different currencies. Jack's second idea was to arrange the stamps by colour and size, but he decided that would be boring. In the end, he arranged the stamps by continent and country, and when he showed the album to his mother, she cried and gave him a hug.

The comprehension questions Mr. Ryan wrote on the board were pretty easy, and even without Billy and Marla's help, Belman thought he could have figured out the answers. After the questions were done, though, each table had to discuss something that they collected and why the collection was important. Belman enjoyed this assignment more. Then, everyone had to stand up at their desk and talk about what they collected, and Belman told the class about a box of action figures he found in the basement after his father moved out.

"My dad said they were called Adventure People by Fisher Price. All of his friends played with Star Wars and Battlestar Galactica figures, but he liked the Adventure People better. He said they drove cars and rode in canoes and sailboats, but mostly they were just like regular people."

————

Unless it was raining, the gifted students were expected to go outside for half an hour after lunch. And since it wasn't raining, Marla and Belman walked around watching their classmates. Billy Pace and a bunch of boys had stolen some crayons from the arts supplies box, and they were peeling the paper off each one. Afterwards, Billy laid the crayons end to end so he could spell out his name. Since it was June, he said, it was hot enough to melt the crayons, and his name would be there all summer.

Marla and Belman drifted away and went to sit against the yellow portable. The portable classroom was used for special education students who didn't have their own teacher, but met with consultants and facilitators who came to the school for a week at a time, sometimes two weeks. Most of Mr. Ryan's class thought it was better to have the same regular teacher every day and that the special education students got a raw deal, but Marla and Belman agreed that there might be advantages to seeing a variety of teachers.

"That's what it's like when you go to junior high and high school and university," Marla pointed out. "This way, you'd be used to having many different teachers."

Belman picked a blade of grass and nodded.

Leaning against the portable, they could see the staff parking lot, where some of the Wellington Elementary staff sat in their cars smoking, as if no one had ever told them about carcinogens. Past the cars, Belman saw Mr. Ryan and Vice Principal Garner standing on the sidewalk, and he pointed them out for Marla.

Mr. Ryan was unwrapping a sandwich from wax paper and nodding about something Vice Principal Garner was saying. When she finished talking, she touched his forearm and he gave her half of his sandwich, which was probably egg salad or cheese because Mr. Ryan was a vegetarian and wouldn't bring turkey or bologna. They stood out by the sidewalk all through the lunch break, but Belman and Marla stopped watching.

"It is rude to stare after all," Marla said.

She asked him if he had a story ready for the afternoon, and he nodded. Afternoon story came right after the lunch bell, and today was the Green Table's turn to present. Much like show and tell in grade one, afternoon story meant standing at the front of the class and making a speech for five minutes, except the students didn't have to bring anything for the Show part, and the Tell part didn't have to be true or anything.

"I get nervous sometimes," Belman said.

Marla touched his forearm the way Vice Principal Garner touched Mr. Ryan's.

"You don't have to be afraid, Belman. Standing at the front of the class is the same as a presentation from our desks really."

Belman nodded.

———

After the one-fifteen bell, Billy volunteered to begin afternoon story, and he explained why his right index finger couldn't extend fully, a story Belman had heard before.

"When I was little and I was still crawling, I would get into trouble all the time. My parents tell me that I was always naturally curious. One time I pushed the door to the garage open and fell down three stairs and hit my mother's Buick. Another time I crawled into the cabinet where we keep the pots in the kitchen, and my mother couldn't find me for an hour. On the day I hurt my finger, my mother was making Campbell's tomato soup for lunch. She opened the lid with a can opener, but she only went most of the way around the top. She bent back the lid and poured out the soup, then bent the lid back down and put the can in the garbage."

While Billy broke off from his story to explain why he

preferred chicken noodle soup over tomato, Belman let his mind wander, and he looked above the blackboard at the front of the room. Over Billy's head, there were yellow cardboard pictures of punctuation marks that Mr. Ryan had put up there at the beginning of the year. The period had thick black eyebrows that made it look stern and angry, and the comma smirked like everything would always be all right. The quotation marks were a pair of twin boys with their arms across their chests; they were probably fraternal twins, Belman thought, because they didn't look exactly alike.

"I know Mr. Ryan doesn't eat chicken," Billy continued, "because he's a vegetarian, but my parents say that we have to eat meat because that's the only way we get the protein we need."

Mr. Ryan smiled and nodded.

"So I was crawling, and I guess I am naturally curious, because I got into the garbage bag on the floor. I stuck my finger in the can, but when I tried to pull it out, it got caught on the bent-in lid right near the top knuckle part. And the more I tried to pull it out, the more the lid cut into my finger. After a while, my finger was all cut up and bloody. My father says the tip of my finger was only held on by a small piece of skin, but my mother says the lid didn't cut through the bone, only muscle."

The students groaned, and Billy held up his finger sideways for the class to see.

"The doctor fixed me, but the end of my finger will be a little bit bent-down for the rest of my life."

He paused and smiled.

"That's the end," he said.

Mr. Ryan led the class in applause and asked Marla to come up and share her story. At the blackboard, she stood up straight and held her hands together in front of her.

"Last weekend, my parents took me to the McCullin Organic Farm, which is located thirty minutes northwest of Toronto, just outside the municipality of Brampton."

She'd asked Belman to listen to her practise the story at lunchtime, so he knew what she was going to say. Not only was her recitation well rehearsed, the story was pretty good too. It built from her sampling three different kinds of cheeses in the farm showroom to taking a hayride behind a chestnut-brown mare, and then, at the end, Marla described how she got to hold a soft, yellow baby chick in her hands.

Belman looked at the punctuation pictures again. The parentheses were a boy and girl holding hands, and he wondered if they were really a couple or if they just dated casually.

The class clapped at the end of Marla's afternoon story and she leaned forward at the waist for a modest bow.

"Belman?" Mr. Ryan smiled.

Standing at the front of the room, Belman could smell the tuna-fish salad someone had brought for lunch, and his stomach hurt. He looked toward the back of the room to try and see Marla, but someone's head at the Mauve Table was blocking his view.

"Uhm, a long time ago, there was this couple called Orpheus and Eurydice."

He slowed down to make sure he pronounced the names the way his father had told him to.

"Eurydice was the wife, but she was bitten by a snake and died. Orpheus loved her a lot and so he cried a lot after she was gone. He was so sad that he even started singing sad songs."

A girl at the Blue Table gave Belman a skeptical look that made him falter.

"Because that's what they did when they were really sad a long time ago, they sang songs."

He looked at Mr. Ryan who nodded for him to continue.

"So Orpheus sang so much that God decided to let him come to heaven and get his wife back. God told him that he had to walk in front of Eurydice on the way back to earth, though, and he wasn't allowed to look back at his wife. So Orpheus went to heaven and he found his wife, but as they were walking back to earth, he did turn around and she disappeared."

When Belman had asked his father why Orpheus would turn around, his father had shaken his head and shrugged his shoulders. Then he said he supposed Orpheus was just worried about her.

"The end," Belman said.

The class clapped, but Belman thought they'd probably liked Billy's and Marla's stories better. Billy's had violence and Marla's was sweet. Belman wasn't sure he even understood his own story.

Current events usually came after afternoon story, but as today was the last day of the school year, Mr. Ryan surprised the class with a chocolate and vanilla marble cake, and gave them all key rings with their names on them. Most of the class got a brown leatherette key ring with their names embossed in metal, but Belman's was different. Mr. Ryan said he looked and looked for one with Belman's name but he didn't have any luck, so in the end, he had one specially engraved.

Belman held out both his hands as the teacher presented it to him.

"That's grand, Mr. Ryan."

————

After the three-fifteen bell, Belman stood with Marla while she waited for her bus, and they talked about what they would do for summer vacation. She was going to horse-lover's camp for two weeks, but she said she'd be back by the end of July. She'd ask if Belman could come over sometimes. They could go for a swim together in the family's pool. Belman smiled and waved with both hands when her bus drove away.

Alone, he leaned against the school and watched for his mother's car. It was a blue Sunfire, and there were lots of them on the road, so he had to watch closely. Remembering the crayons Billy had laid out at lunch, Belman walked behind the technical arts wing, but all he found was a puddle of melted wax, swirled with orange, blue, and green.

He looked at the staff parking lot, which was nearly empty when Mr. Ryan and Vice Principal Garner came out. She was walking fast ahead of him, and it looked like he was trying to keep up. Mr. Ryan said he was sorry and Vice Principal Garner said she should have known better than to get involved with a younger man. He apologized again while she fumbled with her keys and tried to open her car door. She told him he was a child, and said it like it was a swear word.

After her car pulled away, Mr. Ryan looked up and saw Belman. The teacher smiled and shrugged. Belman shrugged back. Although he liked Mr. Ryan a whole lot, Belman was already thinking about grade three.

# S. KENNEDY SOBOL

## SOME LIGHT DOWN

Len Creighton killed Mandy Stevens in 1978, the same year that sugar maples all over the county produced so much sap that its coursing through the lines was audible. In 1981, Meredith Owens disappeared while pine cones and acorns dropped heavy to the ground. Casey Brady was gone three years after that, and when she didn't come back they planted a single locust tree at her elementary school, by the senior doors, where its curled seed pods now collect in the eaves like a tangle of question marks. The year my friend Anna disappeared, we watched tent caterpillars writhing black in their gauzy nests, and blowtorch flames glowing blue-white at dusk as the nests fell away from the trees in clumps, all up and down the street.

Ours was the last in a row of houses on a ridge overlooking the highway. I fell asleep each night with the sound of cars going by below my window, in a room full of brightly coloured objects, which from May to November were covered in a thin layer of dust – a yellow table, a lamp in the corner with an orange paper shade, aquamarine curtains. Even the house's red siding appeared pink under the cloudy haze that clung to it in spite of the wind that whipped across the open road. The year I turned sixteen, the apple trees held their blossoms stubbornly, until I woke one morning in early June and the petals had fallen, papering the ground with white. I went downstairs and sat in the kitchen with my father and my younger sister, Felice. There was an extra plate in the centre of the table, holding a single fried egg heaped with a mound of salt. My sister had fallen prey to our father's favourite joke – the loosened cap on the salt shaker.

"You two waste more eggs," our mother said.

"This was my dream," said Felice. "A boa constrictor was hidden in the walls of the house. It was turning itself inside out in there, so you and Mom and I were trying to find it and get it out."

"Where was Cookie?" my dad said.

"She was packing everything we have into boxes. She wanted us to move and leave the house forever, with the snake still in it."

My mother listened as she swept, along the base of the counters, and under the table where we sat. She batted gently at the tops of our feet with the broom, the way she did when Felice and I were little and made forts out of the tables and chairs on snow days.

"Where are my girls?" she would say to the room as she poked around, pretending not to hear us giggling. "I swear, if I don't find them soon I'll cry and cry. I'll be inconsolable. They'll have to fish me out from the depths of the river."

Felice told me once that this last line always made her

picture our mother not drowned or drowning, but hiding –
huddled in a ball underwater, legs tucked up to her chest and
toes gripping some seaweed to keep from floating to the top.

"It's not dark down there," Felice said. "Everything is
glowing. The seaweed is swirling all around her. It tickles her
and she's laughing a little, with bubbles curling up over her
cheeks. It's just a trick she's playing, hiding from us the way we
hid from her."

In the kitchen, the phone rang and my father lifted both his
hands, showing fingertips stuck all over with butter and toast
crumbs, absolving himself of any phone-answering responsibilities. Mom answered and, as she listened, her face changed.
She turned away from me, and I knew.

"Cookie," she said to me after hanging up. "They found
her."

I knew that she meant her body, but for a few seconds I pictured Anna in the scene I made up four years earlier, when she
disappeared – far away and actually alive, sitting with a happy
family at the kitchen table in the morning. In this picture,
there are palm trees swaying outside the window. From where
Anna sits, you can even see the ocean.

Suddenly the curtains above our kitchen sink unruffled and
were sucked back, flat against the screen. The sun shone
through the thin yellow panels and then they billowed out
again, revealing the highway and the car lot on the other side,
tucked into the corner of the field where Anna and I met every
morning before school. Shallow ditches stretched fully across
its width, the mounds between them evenly spaced, like an
enormous patch of corduroy. It seemed as though the dust had
lifted and I couldn't breathe.

**A loaf of bread, a container of milk, and a stick of butter**
You always hear people say it – they lived next door, down the street. We never imagined. All this time. There was Len, and there was his wife, Linda. What did she know? As I have learned, the clues were scant. When you gather them up, pencil smudges on scraps of paper, you have something, nothing. It was all interference and static, messages never received. Trails covered with fallen branches and dry leaves.

**The Mystery Machine**
Underneath the open window on the second floor, the view from Felice's bed was almost wholly blocked by the maple tree, full of bright green leaves and hung with bell-like clusters of tender, yellow maple keys. I leaned against the sill, picking at the white paint where it was peeling away from the wood in dusty curls.

"You've lost something," she said. "Now you have to retrace your steps."

Felice is an expert at mysteries. When she started kindergarten she was in the afternoon class until she realized that she was missing *Spider-Man*, and made Mom switch her into the morning class. She still watches *Scooby-Doo, Where Are You?* every day after school, finding patterns in the plots and mapping them out against the more famous and complicated mysteries they might be lifted from.

"You know when you're typing," she said, "and you accidentally hit the letters to one side of each of those you meant to? There's a word in there like a secret you're keeping from yourself. Just start from the start."

Anna and I were twelve when she disappeared, the same age Felice was the year they found Anna. We had been getting ready for confirmation. Anna and I had our saint names picked out from the time we were in grade six, when we used to make up stories featuring our saints as competing heroes. Anna's was Catherine of Alexandria, suggested to her by her mother in the hopes that she would not choose wrongly when selecting a husband. I chose Saint Zita, patron saint of bakers and servants, for whom angels had baked loaves of bread while she was in fits of rapture. Angels had also helped Catherine of Alexandria, carrying her body to the top of Mt. Sinai, so in Anna's stories she was always lifted away from danger at the last moment, up and out of the scene, though in Anna's stories the saint always remained alive.

One Saturday, I went to meet Anna in the field, and waited there for half an hour before deciding to go to the Dominion, where her mom worked on weekends. Cardboard boxes were piled high behind the windows, and birds were skipping in and out among the shopping carts that lined the front wall. Anna's mom was at the convenience counter, filling up the container of courtesy matches beside the cash register.

"She damn well better be there," she said, flipping over every second matchbook so that they alternated, top to bottom, bottom to top. "Her Aunt Sharon's coming over this afternoon to measure her for her dress."

A customer waiting for cigarettes started drumming his fingers on the counter, so I turned to go. Over my shoulder, I heard her shout out my name, but I pretended to be interested in a display of Easter Creme Eggs. I heard her swearing under her breath, so I turned and walked quickly towards the exit. By the doors, there was a pen dispenser in with the gum machines, full of plastic pens the same colours as rainbow Chiclets: lime peel, magenta, and yellow, all arranged in a circle like the thing they brought out sometimes in church, with gold and silver tines streaming out from it like the rays of the sun. I put in a quarter and got a pen that was dark lilac. I tore a corner off one of the cardboard boxes and tried to write a note, but the ink wore thin almost right away and I had to make letters by poking holes with the pen, so when it was done you could only read what I had written by connecting the dots.

I ran back to Anna's place. She lived in a red-brick building above some shops on the main street. To get there you had to go up the back stairs and across the gravel-covered first-floor roof. The tenants had divided it up using clotheslines and makeshift fences to form yards. There was no answer at the door, so I went to Anna's window, pressing my forehead against the glass. I opened the window and climbed in.

We had started leaving notes under each other's pillows around the same time we developed our superstition about the tooth fairy. It was Anna's idea that if you gave your teeth away, the rest of you may follow (and even worse, no one would mourn your absence, as though you had agreed to some kind of deal). So it wasn't worth the nickel or whatever you would get. Instead we traded our baby teeth with each other. When one of us lost a tooth, it was the other's turn to come up with one to exchange. One time at school we discovered that I had a grey tooth. I was already one tooth ahead of Anna, so I sat in class all day pushing up with my tongue to keep it in place. I kept her teeth beside my bed in a container I had made out of DAS modelling clay, and she kept mine in a little blue tin that she had painted with a pattern of dragons, tails and necks intertwining.

## Flood

I'd heard the story of the flood so many times, with so many variations, that there were details I was no longer certain were real. Every year Ed from the post office came to our school and gave a talk, followed by film footage taken on the day it happened in 1954. We saw people running through ankle-deep water and, later, the fibreglass figures from the Nativity scene, left out too long, floating past the Dairy Bar without a sound – kings and an angel and donkeys and lambs, all out of proportion to one another. Ed described the volunteer fire-fighters piling sandbags outside the Feed 'N' Seed, and the rowboat he used to make his way across town. Once he told us about Ellie Creighton, the woman who died, trapped in her cellar as the waters pressed in. I went to the post office, to see if he could tell me more. He knew everything about this place, so I secretly hoped that he could tell me something about Anna as well.

"Come on around back," Ed called over his shoulder. He had a soft and reassuring voice that reminded me of the cool tiles on classroom floors. I lifted up the hinged section of the counter and he pointed me towards a folding chair, then disappeared around the corner. The chair faced the back of the post office boxes – a wall of cells gleaming like a giant silver honeycomb. Small doors opened from the other side, and the faint voices of two women carried across the narrow tunnels.

"Well, this is it."

"Mind you, they say he was quite a drinker when he was a young lad."

Ed came back around the corner. "Something here for you."

He dropped a brown envelope on the table. *Ministry of Transportation*.

"Oh," I said. "My driver's licence." Now I could go anywhere.

The women were still talking.

"Just teeth," one was saying, and in my mind I could see them, lined up in the crease at the bottom of an evidence bag: yellow, ivory, and grey. I knew them. Held up to the light they would look like little beads, glossy and of uneven thickness.

## The dumb waiter

It wasn't a secret. There were others, and all of us knew it. Three girls we didn't know, missing from three towns we hardly ever went to. Their absence was like the speed of the river in spring, or the darker spots that marred its frozen surface in winter. It fell into that kind of category. A dangerous and thrilling backdrop that we never took as seriously as we could have.

In my room I opened the envelope that contained my driver's licence and slid the card into my wallet. From the drawer of my bedside table I took a pen, a small tape recorder, and a notebook left over from my *Harriet the Spy* days. I flipped through it to see if there were enough blank pages. It was half empty, and the last entry was in Anna's handwriting. *Jason O'Donnell is a rat fink*, it said, and underneath she had drawn a picture of him in a striped T-shirt and high-tops, with a halo of hearts spinning wildly away from his head. I turned the page. On the other side the ink was showing through, and I tucked my pen in against the spine.

## Casey Brady, 1984

I found someone who knew Casey Brady, the third girl to disappear. We sat in her living room, in a cream-coloured bungalow on Franktown Road. I pulled the tape recorder from my bag and pressed record.

So that year there were boys. And no frog-catching contests, obviously. There was dancing later, and tinny music on a grey plastic ghetto blaster. On one side of Casey's house was the river, and on the other a three-way intersection that marked the south edge of town. The house next door to hers had a small guardrail on the front lawn, because so many cars had crashed through their porch and into their living room in the middle of the night.

The year before, we had all been there together, at what would be the last all-girl birthday party. Casey's mother organized a frog-catching contest. We scattered. One of the girls came back carrying a giant water-logged rat in a wooden salad bowl. There was a huge commotion as Casey's mother despaired that the bowl was ruined and had to be thrown out.

Now things were different. Casey's parents were divorced and phoning it in. Not all of us got along the same way we once did. Or, we did, but things changed faster, with people constantly grouping and regrouping, abandoning plans. I paid less attention than I used to. The water was high and we assembled on a large stretch of flat rock between the grass and the river. Casey walked down the bank towards us with arms full of marshmallows. Gold earrings dangled from her freckled earlobes, and her curly orange hair was bright against the woods behind her, where the space between the elms was darkening.

We poured twenty-sixers and two-litre pops into a large plastic vat indiscriminately, scooping it up with clear plastic cups that kept breaking. We drank until we were like blind animals. In the night, we lost track and spread out across the lot. Joanne walked straight into a tree. I wandered off and found Corey Conley with his hand in his shorts, lying on his back in the moss. Then I was on my hands and knees throwing up bright pink between two skinny tree trunks when someone started rubbing my back. I batted their arm away because it was making me sicker.

When we woke up in the morning, Casey was gone. We tore around everywhere, through the cattails and prickly ash. We cried, we called her older brother and waited. We thought that she had drowned.

### Silver teeth, fox

Anna's family moved to town in the middle of fourth grade, plunking her down among us in a January of heavy snow and blinding light. The sidewalk between our school and the arena had not been shovelled in weeks, so we walked along the road. The wind was so strong that icicles froze at slight angles, and we lost our footing on patches of compressed snow that glared silver in the bright sun.

At the rink, I sat struggling to tighten my stiff leather skates under a wide window that faced out onto the ice. Anna walked past, balancing on her picks and making a grinding sound as she moved across the concrete, arms held away from her sides for balance. She was wearing pink from head to toe – pink skirt and tights and sweater set, with matching pink Fun Fur mittens and earmuffs, all the same colour as the soft downy tissue of a rabbit's ear. Once on the ice, I edged forward by moving my feet laterally, trying to lift my blades as little as possible. Anna sped by me several times, her momentum causing me to teeter backwards in her wake, waving my arms at my sides in an attempt to remain upright. Even in borrowed skates, she finished her laps before anyone else in grade four.

When the buses came at the end of the day, an announcement was made. There was a rabid fox in town, so all town kids had to be picked up. As I packed my book bag, Ms. Clark steered Anna towards me.

"Your parents aren't home, Cookie," said Ms. Clark. "So you'll be going to Anna's farm until they can come get you."

"You have a farm?" I said to Anna.

"My grandfather's," she said.

"Where is your place?"

"We all live there," she said. "We're getting back on our feet." I pictured a family of turtles, weebling upside down in their shells, small legs swimming helplessly in the air.

Anna's grandfather drove slowly, and Anna said that when we got there, we could play *Don't Cook Your Goose*. From somewhere inside her grey wool coat she produced a pink flannel bag full of Lik-M-Aid and Kraft caramels, Bazooka gum and Pixy Stix. I pressed the heel of my hand against the window of the pickup truck, melting away a section of frost and revealing the fields beyond. The fox was out there, all alone, fur faded and skinny, mad. I breathed into the space cleared by my palm, and the glass slowly filled with spiralling triangles of ice, thin as paper.

## Mandy Stevens, 1978
A newspaper article from that year led me to Tyler McLean, who worked with Mandy Stevens the summer after grade twelve.

I was scooping dead frogs out of the pool filter when my older sister told me that Mandy was gone. There were four frogs in the pile already, flat and rotting.

"Pretty funny she should disappear on her way to meet someone likely going to kill her one of these days anyway," she said. My sister had her husband run off on her three weeks before, and her with the two kids, so she was pretty much unsympathetic.

"Yeah," I said. "Real funny."

The frog pile was moving. There was one near the bottom that was still alive and trying to pull itself out from under the rest of them. I thought about it, then left it there.

Mandy was superstitious, always counting things.

Our first day out she asked me if I remembered graph paper.

"Yeah I *remember* it," I said, but if she thought it was a stupid question she didn't let on.

Our job was to survey cottagers for the Conservation Authority, measure the distances between their well and septic and the shoreline. We spent the summer touring the back roads, working in the morning then fucking off for the afternoons because it was the only way to make the work stretch over the length of the contract. My father had a kind of tree collection, birch trees and poplars and red maples. Sometimes we would go sit on his screened-in porch and all you could see was the leaves, closing us in.

One morning we were driving and there was a snapping sound under the truck. She looked up at me with those wide eyes. I pulled over and got out, trying to swear quietly enough that she couldn't hear me. We had torn a hole in the oil pan, and it was emptying out fast.

She toed the ground where the oil was clumping in the sand.

As we walked towards the highway, her arm kept brushing up against mine, and she asked me if there were bears. I told her a black bear would only run away from us. We finally made it to a garage, got towed, and while we waited I got her a yellow plastic fawn from a vending machine. For the rest of the summer she kept it on a green vinyl string and twirled it constantly around her finger.

I only saw her once after that summer. She was shrieking and carrying on in the middle of the pool hall in town. As I wondered what was happening, Randy Connell abandoned his pinball machine with an upward sweeping motion against its sides and crossed over to her, pressing his cigarette into the soft inside part of her elbow, and she took it so casual I thought I was the only one in there who saw. A second later I wondered if I'd seen it at all. Then she was hysterical, laughing and walking towards the pay phone. I stepped in front of her.

"What?" she said. "Get out of my road."

"What are you doing with that guy?" I said. "He's a fucking loser."

Her face went blank for a second and then she started laughing again and I got confused and I forget what I said after that but when I stopped talking, she stopped laughing. And she squinted at me, like she thought I knew what she was thinking and wasn't letting on. She looked over my shoulder, then, like she saw a ghost, and we were both quiet.

## Noise

My father was repairing the fence at the back of our yard, facing the highway.

"I was on the road a lot," he said. He grasped a piece of thick wire in a pair of pliers and twisted it back and forth until it snapped. He wouldn't turn his attention away from the fence.

"I mostly remember you being home," I said, and I hoped that this would console him. The traffic on the highway was light for a few moments, and in the distance you could hear the faint hum and click of the drive-through intercoms at the fast-food restaurants. Every one of them has at least one frequency pairing – a customer number and a clerk number that you can use to listen to people placing and receiving orders. Tim Hortons is 30.5800/154.4900, Burger King is 30.8400/154.5700, and Dairy Queen is 457.5750/467.8000. My father used to haul freight, and if he was home on Friday nights after *Dallas*, he would pile Felice and I into the cab of the truck in the driveway, blankets and all. We listened to people's orders, switching back and forth between the Dairy Queen and the Burger King and trying to guess who the voices belonged to. Once, as I drifted off, I heard a rush of crackling sounds, like a river of static tumbling over rocks, then one last order, a man asking for kids' meals. Five of them. One with each type of prize, if possible.

## Meredith Owens, 1981

Meredith Owens' family had kind of lost touch with her in the months before she went missing. She went to an alternative high school and got student welfare. They lived in the same town, but barely spoke to each other. A mural she painted is still visible on the side of a local chip wagon there, illustrating a pair of chipmunks eating a picnic lunch on a tree stump, under a faded rainbow. She had a cousin, who is now a doctor.

The fingerprints on Meredith's thumb and index finger were cracked and distorted from the time when she was three and stuck a pair of tweezers in an electrical outlet. She had ashy blond hair and loved orange, and often gave her belongings away. She had a charm bracelet that she always wore, and whenever anyone said they liked it, she would take a charm right off and give it to them.

The last time I saw her she showed me her arm. She had just been to the allergist's and it was marked with a grid of tiny red flecks, where minuscule triangles of skin had been torn away using a small metal pick, and concentrated allergens applied with an eye dropper. Swollen weals dotted the rows, ragged-edged blotches of pink and flattish puffs the colour of her skin, like mosquito bites. She pointed at each of them saying, this is mould, this is cut grass, this is another type of mould. There was one near her wrist that she couldn't stop scratching. This was three days before.

## Rewinding

We each had our favourite parts of Ed's school visits. Felice's was the part of the story when the flood waters calmed, and they sat on their roofs for hours, watching fish swimming underfoot, darting along the eaves and poking their tiny round mouths out just above the surface of the water. Mine was the section of the film that showed the houses submerged. I would picture the rooms full to their ceilings with water, like aquariums, curtains swaying like seaweed in the current. Anna's favourite part was the end, when Ed rewound the film with the projector light still on, and we watched the water recede, the clouds darken and fade, birds light on the tips of tree branches, black against the white sky.

## Vesica piscis

My mother was in the living room, wiping the dust from the mantle, the turntable. I asked her if she remembered the time she thought we were gone. Felice was six, writing lemon juice messages on old sheets of foolscap, then holding them over a candle to reveal the words. We were in the basement, and I watched as she left a piece of paper over the flame too long, and it caught. It was winter and she started running with the paper up the stairs. At the top, she flung open the side door and thrust her arm out far enough that the fire, when released, would not fly back into the house. The flames were swallowed by a snow bank, leaving only a small piece of the page on which writing was visible. Melted snow seeped through the paper, muddying the lines, making the ink swell and overflow the banks of each letter, filling every loop and curl.

As we crouched on the step watching the secret words darken and blur, we heard yelling from a few houses down, and Felice put one finger to her lips. We went back into the house for our boots and coats, slunk to the far edge of our yard and then along the neighbour's rear fence to listen, hidden. In the clear, cold day, their voices sounded like they were wrapped in glass, each with a different sound, like a chime or a xylophone key.

Ten minutes later we were back in the house, filling a cup with juice from a plastic lemon, when my mother ran in from outside. The door slammed. She was out of breath and we could see that she was scared.

"Where were you?" she screamed.

I asked her if she had known about Len.

"No," she said, and then she told me, as she dusted, about a fourth missing girl.

In December of 1975, two weeks before I was born, forty-three children stood dressed as birds at the front of the church, in costumes made of garbage bags. They had cut feathers out of coloured tissue paper and taped them on in rows, and pinned yellow construction paper beaks to their toques and hoods. Standing in tiers on the steps around the altar, they waited for their cue to begin, creating a soft rustle as they breathed.

My mother and father sat perched in the balcony. They had never had a child before, and in those days they watched their surroundings with fear and excitement, as though the world itself were a prologue to an entirely new one that was about to be revealed, forming out of everything around them. The lights went down and my father squeezed my mother's hand.

A spotlight appeared on a group of snow buntings, who introduced the story with a four-line song. Then the whole stage was lit, revealing blue jays and cardinals, tanagers and swallows and warblers of all kinds, each with markings rendered in layered sections of translucent paper around their arms and throats. The smallest children were dressed as chickadees with black toques on their round heads, and once their part was over, they sat directly on the floor beneath them, some falling asleep on the red carpet. Periodically, one of them would get up abruptly and run down the aisle, returning to their parents as though released from a spell.

As the finale began, Ms. Clark indicated with one upraised arm that the audience should stand and join in. The lights were lowered again and the children, singing, made their way through the dark to the back of the church, some with flash-lights, the older ones with candles that kept going out in the draft. The buntings and swallows criss-crossed through the procession, arms outstretched, knocking into each other until the aisle was finally empty, the song ended, and the lights were turned back on. Everyone milled towards the back, parents assembling with ski jackets held open like nets with which they could recapture their children.

As my parents descended the staircase, my father kept twisting around to make sure that my mother's feet landed squarely on each and every step. They heard scuffling below, then several voices that grew louder and louder. A child's name was repeated over and over again – at first it was a question mark, then an exclamation point, then a question mark again. There was an interval of silence before everyone realized that something was wrong. As they searched for the girl, a set of tarnished gold fans spun overhead, and her name was called over and over again, across a bright shifting sea of tissue-paper feathers.

**A row of houses**
"For you," Felice said, handing me a note written on pink and mauve dollar-store stationery. There was an illustration of a basket of flowers on the top and a ribbon along the border, woven under and over the lines on the page.

"It was in the mailbox," she said. "Note the circles used to dot the 'i's."

I looked out the window, across the highway. Linda was in the car lot, polishing an old Hertz van that had a huge band of black covering the name on the side.

One night a couple of years before, Linda had come to our door. It was January, and in some places the snowdrifts swept over the tops of fences – soft, deep waves of blue under the dome of light that spread from the highway and the town behind it. She stood there in her parka and a felt skirt, with clumps of snow spilling into the tops of her boots, melting against her nylons. All of her clothes looked like she made them herself – matching two-piece sets in a stiff fabric that was constantly shifting around her body, with puffed-out seams as though the front and back panels were pasted together and hung over her shoulders, like she was a paper doll.

She asked if our phone was working and Felice told me to go check, never letting her eyes off Linda, and not moving at all to allow her in. She was in a phase where she did this to everyone, mentally committing their facial features to memory like she was taking down the licence plate of a suspicious car. I came back with the cordless phone and squeezed between Felice and the door, opening it wider to let Linda through. Felice shrugged her shoulders and we all sat at the kitchen table while Linda made her phone call. When she was done she told us that she was alone over there.

"Len goes to Florida every year," she said. Felice asked why she didn't go with him.

"Oh you know," she said. "I'm not one for the sun. And someone has to run the lot."

She cleared her throat.

"I used to watch you two tobogganing," she said. "'Those kids,' I used to say to Len. 'It's lucky for them the fence is there, lest they find themselves flying right out into the road.'"

A week later, we saw that Len was back, his skin all tanned and leathery, and there was a thank-you note in our mailbox written in round bubbly letters, with a star above the "i" in Linda.

## Jars

A week after they found Anna, I met Linda at the Dairy Queen, where she swamped me with an endless supply of Len-always-saids.

"'Odometers can be turned back,' he would say. 'If you don't know that, I don't feel sorry for you.' I didn't really like that," Linda said.

Linda fidgeted while everything around her was still, and her mouth in particular seemed never to stop moving. She kept jumping up in the middle of sentences to go to the counter. I focused on the sound of the Blizzard machine. The table was littered with glassine paper wrappers, square pouches with patches of red and yellow diamonds on the front.

"You got my note," she said, but we had already been talking for ten minutes.

We sat in a booth, and she bought me a Dilly bar and a chili dog. I didn't want either of them, or at least I wished that she had got the chili dog first, instead of the other way around. Also, I wished that I wasn't there talking to her at all. The more she spoke, the more I felt the past rearranging itself, and retroactive panic as she filled in the gaps. She slid a paper cup full of water back and forth across the table, saying that she had already told everything to the police, but that she thought someone should talk to me directly before it all got out.

It was Linda who led the police to Len's childhood home, which was not a home at all but a bump in the ground, an oak tree, and sections of an old fence. The cellar door stuck only a little, and Linda stumbled a bit on the steps, but then they saw. Narrow shelves stood floor to ceiling, made of two-by-sixes that seemed to be embedded in the dirt walls, holding row upon row of old mason jars. She walked closer, tracing her fingers over raised glass letters, peering inside and seeing: a yellow plastic fawn, some gold earrings, a white paper feather. There was a blue tin with dragons painted on it, a charm bracelet, and among a hundred other trinkets glowing bright, five jars that held nothing but ashes.

## Frog catching

We went frog catching in the park. Really I did all of the catching; Anna couldn't pick them up. The instant she felt their hearts and lungs pulsing, her cupped hands would spring open, sending the frog soaring with one leg dangling behind as it scrambled in the air. Once, we found a dead frog with a white and bloated tongue stretched far ahead of his deflated body.

"It looks like someone shoved a piece of macaroni down his throat," Anna said, and started crying.

"Hey," I said, "he was a macaroni of the 18th century." It was a line in a book we had read. She started laughing. Then I started laughing, then crying, both of us bent forward with our hands on our knees to steady ourselves.

## Vanishing Point

Once I thought of leaving this place. Dad had been out on the road for two weeks. He called one night in July, and Mom talked to him as the three of us sat at the kitchen table. She listened, smiling sweetly as though he were right there in front of her, and then tilted the receiver away from her mouth.

"He says Abbott and Costello are on satellite at the motel."

Felice laughed. When we were small, our father told us each a new bedtime story every single night.

"Choose three things," he would say, and then he'd assemble the story around them. The stories were always different, even though the ingredients were often the same. For the longest time, Felice almost always chose a hollow log, a bag of marbles, and a talking rabbit or lynx. Then one Saturday we watched *Abbott and Costello Meet Frankenstein*, and from that time on, all her stories included a house with a hidden room, behind a secret revolving door.

"Come home in one piece," my mother said into the phone.

"How else," said Felice, and she pulled apart a Lego man she'd been working on. "What have you got here?" she said to me, pulling from behind my ear our favourite piece – the translucent trapezoid. "Wouldn't he look nice with a windshield for a head?"

The next morning I got up early and crossed the highway. A wire fence ran perpendicular to the highway, and birds sat gently bobbing all along it, some clutching their feet to the rectangular cells for just a moment before passing through. After an hour of waiting and holding my thumb out I began to picture myself from a distance – on the horizon, not moving but shimmering, shimmering until I disappeared.

I heard footsteps behind me, and turned around.

"You want to take a look at the car?" said Len. "The one you and your friend like so much?"

"That's my sister," I said. My head felt heavy from the heat of the sun.

There was a month when I was ten during which Felice and I came to look at the car whenever we could, our favourite because there were clear orange dice atop the lock pulls. Sometimes Len would come out of his office and tell us not to touch it; other times he would describe its features to us as though we were real customers.

Suddenly I was dizzy, and felt myself stumbling down one side of the ditch and up the other. Len took a big step forward and caught my arm. Just as he did, a car whipped by on the highway.

"There goes your chance," he said.

"Whatever," I said, staring down the length of the highway as the car receded from view.

"You better sit down in the shade for a minute," he said, opening the door of a copper-coloured Reliant.

It was cool inside on the burgundy velour seats. There were ashes all over the dash, and it smelled like the pink fluoride they make you line up for at school. The car faced the road and I could see my mother in our backyard, kneeling in the garden, framed by the windshield. On the floor there was a muddy map and a 1976 guide to Eastern Ontario. We had one just like it at home, and I'd read it over and over again, trying and failing to find a mention of our town.

"Do you know my wife Linda?" Len was holding a picture

in front of my face, blocking out the scene of my mother in the garden.

"Yes," I said, but this picture was not of the Linda I knew. It was old – square with a white border. There was a woman wearing a bright pink suit jacket and miniskirt, the top of one stocking showing. She was standing in front of what looked like the back of a closet, with wood-veneer panelling. A paint-by-number picture of a sad-eyed dog hung from a coat hook over her shoulder.

"I like to paint," Len said. "I bet you didn't know that."

I thought about how the lot must look from the other side of the road. From my sister's window, for example, it would waver silver in the heat. I'd be invisible in this picture, hidden behind a reflection of the sky.

My elbow was on the vinyl armrest that was pulled down between the two seats. I felt it tugging at the skin on my arm, my palms were sweaty, then his hand was on my leg and he wasn't taking the picture away. Suddenly I was in motion, my right shoulder pressing against the door as I pulled the handle towards me. I ran across the highway without looking, some-thing I'd been warned all my life not to do. As I neared my house, the smell of fried zucchini coming from next door made my stomach fold in on itself, and my mother, fussing over green tomatoes that were camouflaged among their own leaves, leaned back and looked at me.

"What have you been doing?" she said.

"Nothing."

In the space between my foot and one of the rocks that bor-dered the vegetable garden there were shiny black crickets moving along with their funny horizontal hops, legs sweeping together like tiny barbed scissors.

"Okay," she said.

I opened the side door and stood at the top of the stairs that led down to the cool basement. My sister was sitting on the bottom step, practising magic tricks. "Hold out your hand," she said.

## Eluviation

That day at the post office, Ed said that I hadn't imagined the part about the lady who died. He had told us about it just once, the year we were in grade six, but seeing our distress decided never to mention it again.

"When they found Ellie Creighton," he said, "her son Len was there. The cellar doors burst open and everything in the basement spilled out – Ellie and a broken chair and everything in her pantry. I remember she had a brooch on her sweater. I think he kept it."

I tried to picture it, cans and mason jars and bloated boxes of pancake mix spread all over the water-logged yard, and Len, unfastening the brooch from her sweater, bits of dirt and rust falling down the sides of a mason jar as he unscrewed the lid, dropping the brooch inside. And I knew, because I had seen it, that where there once was a house, now there was nothing. Just a mound of sod that half-concealed a cellar door, and an oak tree that had grown around a page wire fence, with thin metal tangles curling back towards the trunk, and the tree's many strands of bark tapering into a few just above the fence, like a dart in a mitten.

## Ashes

After all the evidence was processed, a funeral was finally held for Anna. At the church hall afterwards, we ate pieces of coconut cream pie off flimsy paper plates. In the kitchen, the Women's League ladies and their daughters were chirping around a huge table that took up most of the room, covered in heavy glass bowls full of green Jell-O with peas, red Jell-O with shredded carrot. Plastic bowls with white pleated lids concealed coleslaw, three-bean salad, devilled eggs. These things were always the same. Wedding, funeral, baptism, confirmation: the same people and the same midday light from the window refracting through the bowls of Jell-O like stained glass.

Felice tugged on my sleeve.

"Mom and Dad said that you could drive me home," she said. "And we could go to the Dairy Queen."

We took the back way, through the parking lot of the box factory, driving around in circles while we ate our ice cream.

Felice turned to me. "Do you think you have all the pieces?"

I wasn't sure. I thought of the art project we did once in Ms. Clark's class. A huge landscape painting that she'd found at a garage sale was cut up into three-by-three-inch squares, and each of us was given pieces of it. We were to paint new squares, imitating the originals, then reassemble the painting. One of Anna's pieces was a section of sky with part of a bird wing in it, and most of mine were from the river, just water from edge to edge. When the paint dried we taped the squares to the wall, following a numbered diagram. In the end it was the same painting, but it wasn't. Every square was painted in a different style, with slightly different colours, creating grid lines that made it difficult to absorb the whole scene at once.

There was a stand of trees near the horizon line, for example, that seemed to be in both the background and the foreground at once, because no one had used the same shades of black and green to paint the shadows among the leaves.

Felice leaned forward, towards the windshield.

"Look," she said. "It's snowing."

Flakes of grey and white were falling from the sky – ashes fluttering from the factory smokestack, filling the circles left by my tires. We saw some light down on the glass, then drift gently aside as the car moved forward.

# SARAH STEINBERG

## AT LAST AT SEA

"My dear, you will love it," my mother had told me over the phone from Toronto, lingering on the L, attending to the V. "You'll just *love* it," she said again, as I wrapped the phone cord around my wrist like a bracelet, staring out at the palm tree in my backyard. "It's just *glorious*. I'll fly in and stay with you, and we'll board the ship from San Diego. You'll see."

But I don't like being in a place where the doors don't lead to land and each day begins and ends like the one before it. No newspapers, no cooking, no cash, and the only thing to see out the window is ocean. Grey, blue, white, and water, water, water. It doesn't even seem that we're moving.

When the elevator reaches the lido deck, the door opens on a gaggle of little kids in bathing suits. One of them, a small girl about five, is wearing orange flotation devices on her arms. I've seen her in the water every day, splashing around and giggling.

"Hi, Fishy," I say, and wave. We had a conversation in the pool yesterday. She explained to me, her eyes big and round and earnest, that she was a dolphin-in-a-whale-fishy-boat. My mother is already making her way toward the buffet. Fishy waves back.

Lounge chairs line the rim of the pool on the lido deck, employed mostly by ladies in old-fashioned bathing suits with oily, rubbery skin, many of whom have positioned sheets of aluminum under their faces to catch the sun. The majority of the ship's passengers appear to be these old ladies, travelling in twos and threes, though there is the occasional husband, plate heaped with food, lingering behind a more ambulatory wife. And there are some younger couples too, celebrating, I can only imagine, first and second anniversaries. I wish my mother had a group of friends to cruise with, to play mah jong with, to talk to.

Across the deck at the buffet, my mother is gesturing to me. She picks up a piece of something from a plate and pops it into her mouth. As she begins to chew, she stabs her finger three times toward the plate, and then at me, and then again at it. I recognize this pantomime. I shake my head no, and then she repeats the same series of gestures. The man beside her is staring. When she points at the food again, thrusting her finger toward it more forcefully, and for the third time, he goes around her.

She is wearing only a purple bathing suit and a straw hat, a pair of enormous sunglasses overwhelming her already small face. I feel embarrassed, but in fact I'm embarrassed to be embarrassed. This is my mother, with the good intentions, the incessant worry ("For your welfare, dear") and the endless, inane stories of minor domestic disturbances (a raccoon-in-the-garbage-can might last up to half an hour, complete with a detailed denouement outlining the steps taken to protect the garbage against another attack). And she is also, at times, poetic, as when she wrote to me in an email about the mother of a bride: "That bitch Anne will be cool and elegant in some invisible little number, and I envision myself sweating, red-faced and thirsty."

My mother is talking to a woman who is also wearing a straw hat, her hair pulled back into a neat bun. This woman is lean and well-dressed, in linen pants and a blousy top. She is perfectly attired for a luxury cruise, though that is not quite what this is. I bob around in the water for a while, my ears just below the surface.

Later, in our tiny room, my mother is sitting on the sofa smoking a cigarette. She tells me she's made a friend.

"Another woman whose daughter hates her," she says. "It's interesting, we were talking about it, and this woman is a sociologist, but she says she doesn't know why her daughter hates her. She said it just happens that way sometimes, and there's nothing you can do about it."

"Maybe your friend the sociologist needs a therapist," I say.

"Maybe *you* do."

"I'm going back to the pool," I say, and walk out of our room, directly toward the casino.

Our first night on the ship we were placed at a dining table with six others: an elderly couple, neither of whom could hear very well, two sisters, both former schoolteachers, and two women named Cathy – friends in their mid-forties, both from San Diego, both blond, both former bombshells.

The dining room was set elegantly, with white cloth draped over the tables, linen stuffed into the wineglasses, and chandeliers, at least seventy of them, above every table, dripping with glass that was not crystal but looked it.

"Well," my mother said, to no one in particular, and inhaled deeply, as if preparing to answer a question that hadn't yet been asked. Both Cathys looked at her.

"Isn't this nice?" she said, exhaling and unfolding a cloth napkin. The Cathys nodded.

"Is this your first time on a cruise?" one of the Cathys, the one with slightly shorter, blonder hair, asked.

"Oh no!" my mother said. "Oh no, no! I sailed to Peru last year. This is, in fact, my fourth cruise. And not to be my last!" She paused. "Unless I pop off suddenly!"

She looked at me and laughed a deep, miserable laugh. I noticed one of the schoolteachers, whose name I had already forgotten, eye her sharply. Oh, fuck off, I thought at the schoolteacher. Just you fuck off.

Our first course was served, a spinach salad with little chunks of canned white asparagus, tomatoes, and bacon, and I began to pick at it, moving the bacon out of the way with my fork.

The same Cathy spoke up. "I've never been to Mexico before. Except T.J. I mean *real* Mexico. But I'm so excited. I hope I can bring back some nice things. It's so cheap."

My mother seemed to have misunderstood Cathy to mean she was concerned about crossing the border with her new

Mexican treasures, and proceeded to launch into an almost frantic explanation of the U.S. customs system, which, she said, was hardly any different from the Canadian one, and she assured Cathy that border patrol was only looking for people who were attempting to transport serious drugs, firearms, or cash.

I watched the teacher as she wielded her knife and fork to cut the spinach into more manageable pieces and then halved the already small tomatoes and speared them onto her fork. She made little "Uh-huh" sounds and nodded, without looking, in my mother's direction.

By dessert, my mother was still talking – to no one in particular, it seemed – about *The Antiques Road Show*, her mouth full of chocolate cake, and a small piece of asparagus clinging to the side of her chin. I had been staring at her for a long time, ready to point at that spot on my own face, but she never looked at me. The elderly couple had, by then, excused themselves, and the schoolteachers were talking quietly, almost whispering, to each other.

"So what are you going to do now?" I asked, as we were drinking our coffee.

"What the hell do you care?" she said. "You're certainly not going to spend any time with me."

"You know," I said, "if you perhaps tried to ask people some fucking *questions* and then waited long enough to listen to their *responses*, you might actually make some fucking *friends*."

"My daughter with her beautiful language and her advice. Thank you, my darling. I will certainly keep that in mind the next time I'm at dinner with a bunch of sullen witches."

Our dinner companions pretended not to hear. Whatever symphony had been piped into the dining room had been turned off.

When I reach the casino, I see the Cathys sitting at the bar. They smile at me as I near.

"Hi, ladies," I say. I'm not sure how to address them.

"Hi," the blonder Cathy says. "We haven't seen you guys at dinner lately."

"Oh," I lie. "We've been eating in our room."

"Your mom's really funny," she says. The other Cathy smiles into her cocktail.

"Yep," I say. And then, because I can think of nothing else, no questions, I shrug and walk away.

I have twenty bucks in my pocket, and I cash it into chips and sit down at the blackjack table. I bet it all on my first hand, which is a blackjack, and my subsequent hands are nearly all winners. Within a half-hour I'm $180 up. The croupier, Dave, is friendly, and what's more, he seems pleased that I'm winning. I feel better than drunk.

"Well," I say, savouring the sound the chips make as I stack and restack them with my thumb and forefinger, and thinking suddenly of an accordion. "I guess you gotta know when to fold 'em."

"OK, good," Dave says. "Good on ya."

"I know, huh?" I say, surprised by my own restraint.

When I return to our cabin, my mother is still sitting on the little blue sofa. The TV is tuned in to the ship's channel, a closed-circuit surveillance camera on the top deck; you can see the tip of the boat's bow, but mostly just what's in front of us. There's no land in sight. But I think we'll be in Acapulco soon, maybe one more day.

Her face is hard set, her jaw clenched, her mouth a frown. She sweeps her eyes over me, from my face to my feet and back up again – a gesture I see teenage girls do a lot – and then she looks away, at the ashtray, her drink. Her eyes are red.

"You are," she says slowly, nodding her head a bit, "a very bad daughter."

She says this as if it were the conclusion to a conversation that had been going on for a long time. And I suppose that, in many ways, it is.

"Uh-huh," I say, but what I really think is that we have a very small room and I wonder if Dave the croupier would like to fuck me and I wonder how late the ship's bars are open. "You have some spinach on your chin," I say, which isn't true.

I close the door behind me and walk down the tiny passage-way, toward the elevator, thinking I'll go to one of the bars. A few doors down I see Fishy, still wearing her bathing suit, her orange flotation devices still attached to her arms.

"Hi, Fishy!" I say.

"No!" she says, shaking her blond head, her damp hair flapping around her face. "No no no, I told you. I'm a whale-in-a-dolphin-in-a-fishy-boat!"

"Oh," I say, as if it is all clear to me now. "I understand. That's very interesting, though, because you know what?"

"What?"

"I'm a dolphin."

"No!" she says, unconvinced, her mouth open, shaking her head. "Nuh-uh."

"Yep," I say. "It's true. I *am* a dolphin. I'm a dolphin in a girl suit. That's why you can't tell right away."

Fishy looks me over carefully. At first I think she is about to laugh, but then her features twist and she wrinkles her nose and shuts her eyes, and when she opens them again they are brimming with salty little tears.

"No, Fishy," I say, alarmed.

But she lets out a loud, terrified wail, all her teeth in view.

"It's OK, it's OK, dolphins are nice."

But she is scared and I don't dare touch her. As she cries, she reaches up toward the handle of her cabin door, but she's too little and she fumbles with it, twisting it in the wrong direction. I hear footsteps and then the door opens, and Fishy is scooped up by her mother and then gone, the door locked quickly behind them.

"Mommy!" I hear the girl cry, and I stand there, still as salt air, but I can't make out any words, just more crying, then her mother, who murmurs, and a few light sobs, and then, later, nothing.

# ANNA LEVENTHAL

## THE POLAR BEAR AT THE MUSEUM

In gym class we have to measure ourselves with calipers to find out how much of our body is made up of pure fat, as if we are bags of microwave popcorn. You are supposed to pinch a wodge of skin in the calipers and measure your belly, thighs, upper arms – all the mayonnaise-coloured, hairless bits. The thickness of the roll of flesh you conjure up tells you how much of you consists of dimpled, subcutaneous lard and how likely you are to die young.

Beth says the calipers look like something from the museum of gynecology. She squeezes her entire biceps, her neck, and encircles her head with the metal jaw, placing each end in her ear like a stethoscope, taking down measurements as she goes. Her body-fat percentage comes out to ninety-eight. I imagine her carved out of butter, two scornful coffee-bean eyes pressed into the head.

Beth is the smartest one, and the funniest. Also the meanest. Hugging her is like embracing a deck of cards, all flat bone and thin edges you could cut yourself on. She likes to talk about beating up Trina James after school, even though Trina is usually scheduled to fight Morgan Fernandez, who wears a tiny crucifix around her neck and has sad, sepia-coloured eyes. Trina also wears a crucifix, but she has buck teeth and bushy eyebrows. We hate her because she is almost as ugly as we are.

Trina asks if we will get her back in the fight. Why don't you grow some more teeth to cover up those gums, says Beth.

Beth and I play outfield so we can smoke behind the bleachers by the racetrack. We don't have cigarettes, but we roll dried bits of things in paper and set them on fire, then lean over and huff the smoke until we feel giddy. Being in the "gifted" class means nobody cares if you can't throw a curveball or run to second base without getting winded, so we hide out until it's time to change back into our plaid-and-corduroy uniforms and throw our big brains around.

We have to take gym class with the regular kids so we don't become conceited or soft. Corey Kowalchuk is a regular kid and so pretty it makes you sad just to look at him and think about how in forty years he'll either be ugly or dead. One time he tells Beth that Mitch Lewis, who is sitting next to him on the workout bench, has a crush on her, and that he jerks off thinking about her every night with the telephone in his hand and calls her just before he comes. Mitch just stares at his white Adidas that look like small spacecraft. Next Corey turns to me and tells me in a bored-sounding voice that Mitch Lewis wants to hump me, but his dick is too small so he's going to tie a broomstick to it and do me until I'm torn and bleeding.

Mitch continues to look at his sneakers, a furious grin on

his face. I am secretly excited that Corey has spoken to me this much.

Corey's parents live down the street from mine, and back in elementary school we used to take the school bus together to the public school downtown, because our parents didn't want to send us to the private school in our neighbourhood in case we grew up to be assholes. We used to sit together at the back of the bus in our DayGlo snowsuits and make up knock-knock jokes about our teachers. One time the school bus hit a massive pothole, and our tiny little kid bodies bounced really high up off the seats, and both of us swore to each other that we could feel the roof of the bus brushing the stiff hair at the top of our heads. A few years after that, Corey started getting high at recess, and I started wearing a bra and listening to musicals, and we mostly stopped talking to each other, unless Corey had some junior-high wastoid like Mitch Lewis he wanted to humiliate. I guess this is something we learned about in life skills class, though I don't remember anything except Ms. Jablonsky putting a condom on a banana.

Trina James may or may not be a slut, but we know for sure that Mary Roberts is. We can tell because she wears short skirts and knee socks and laughs at boys' jokes. Also, she has baby teeth. These teeth clearly belong in the mouth of a precocious eight-month-old – they are fit only for chewing boiled carrots and celery stew – and yet here they are, lining Mary's gums like seed pearls sewn onto red velvet. BJ teeth, Beth calls them, and we all laugh and pretend to know what she means.

Beth is one gutsy lady. That is what Mrs. Chernyk, the art teacher, says when Beth refuses to snap her gum even though Janine Raymond, the school bully, tells her she has to. Janine enjoys the sound of snapping gum and forces entire classes of terrified kids to do it in unison. Beth just glares at her and bares her teeth, which makes her look like an angry koala bear. Janine tells Beth she will beat her up after school, as soon as Beth is done blowing the janitor, her alleged favourite activity. Mary Roberts looks up from her pencil drawing of Teemu Selänne scoring a goal, and snickers. *Go Jets!!!!!!!* it says at the bottom of the page, in letters that look like bolts of lightning. You're next, Roberts, says Janine, and Mary hunches over with her HB pencil and busily starts adding about thirty more exclamation points to her caption. Beth turns and gives me this warm and reassuring smile, like I'm the one about to get the living crap beat out of her by a girl with LIVE EVIL tattooed on her knuckles.

I stand by Beth's locker at three-thirty, sober and brave and so full of resigned, heartsick love I think I am going to rupture. We wait for Janine to appear and curb-stomp Beth into martyrdom with her purple Doc Martens, but Janine never shows up. My devotional ardour deflates into shame, like a run-over volleyball. After all, I snapped my gum along with the rest of them.

You don't even really need to pay to see the bison at the museum. They're right there in the lobby, their great heavy heads all full of sawdust and excelsior and old sweaters; you can stand there all day and stare at them for free. Which is exactly what Beth is trying to do. Our class is supposed to be researching lichens of the Canadian Shield, but so far Beth hasn't even made it past the ticket booth. She is moored to the parquet floor, leaning against our side of the velvet rope like she's waiting to be let into the Oscars, staring.

The bison are mounted mid-charge, glass eyes peering over their shoulders in what I guess is supposed to be terror, running from a group of two-dimensional Native hunters on horseback who are painted on the wall behind them.

Mary Roberts saunters by and glances at her. Hey, check it out, she says, Beth has a boyfriend. Dances-With-Retards hump'um Big Chief Saggenballs. I wait for Beth to spit out some insult or slap Mary's face, but she just stands there, looking kind of skinny and tired, and I suddenly notice she is wearing two different socks. Mary laughs and bounces away.

God, says Beth, you wonder why they didn't just find some real Indians to stuff. Her voice is flat and empty of bitterness.

Tell me again about your dad, I say. Beth lays out one of two stories about him, depending on her mood and who might be listening. Sometimes he's a Mennonite, a war resister who wriggled through the border in the Sixties, with the ashes of his draft card still warm in his pocket, and was then tucked away by her mother's church group. This story is for when Beth and I are lying on her bed, our eyes red from the joint we've finally learned how to smoke. Her voice when she tells it is soft and dreamy, with none of the corrosive acid that's usually there.

When the combination of asbestos insulation and mouse droppings in the church basement set off florid rashes and welts on the young draft dodger's skin, Beth's mother set up a cot in her own basement and offered him whatever semblance of Christian charity she could muster. He thanked her, sneezing and wiping his oozing eyes on a handkerchief embroidered with tiny clocks.

During the day, Beth's mother ran the church group's printing press, turning out pamphlets on the importance of hard work, faith, and chastity, and at night she took camomile tea to the runaway and they discussed their views on the war and the intricacies of their respective faiths. Pretty soon cups of tea became candlelit dinners eaten off tin camping dishes, and the young Menno, who in Beth's stories looked a lot like Keanu Reeves, fell in love with the Catholic woman. Although she loved him too, his minky black hair and carpentry skills, Beth's mother couldn't picture herself married to this man who didn't dance but who sang like a baritone Gordon Lightfoot and could draw freehand drafts of beautiful round, wood-hewn buildings, free of dusky corners where cobwebs and secrets flourished. Neither of them was willing to compromise, and the word *chastity* floated over their relationship, a naphthalene-smelling ghost. After a few months of whispered fights and unbreakable dishes thrown across the room, the draft dodger left for a rural commune in Saskatchewan. Beth's mother threw herself into her work at the printing press, and though her faith in the Holy Trinity was fading, she found comfort in the smell of mimeograph ink.

She heard nothing from the draft dodger for years, until one evening he appeared on her doorstep. I don't have much time, he said, they found me. I've been court-martialled. Tomorrow I'm being smuggled to Paraguay. He still looked like Keanu Reeves, though his hair was longer and straggly and streaky-grey. She let him in. What else could she do? He left early the next morning in a white van with Alaska plates, and Beth's mother never heard from him again.

And nine months later, Beth finishes, I was born.

Wait a second, I say, President Carter pardoned all the war resisters in 1977, so he couldn't have been in real trouble. (I'm not the *Reach for the Top* team captain for nothing.)

Yeah, okay, says Beth, but you had to apply for a pardon, and there was a time limit anyway. He never got his.

Why wouldn't he apply? I ask.

I don't know, because he was getting high on some fucking commune, okay?

I am silent, and Beth slowly exhales a kite's tail of smoke.

Anyway, Beth goes on, you know what the moral is?

No.

A trace of hydrochloride seeps back into her voice. You haven't had a night until you've had a Mennonite.


The other father is for parties when Beth has smoked two or three joints and drunk most of the vodka we've smuggled from my parents' liquor cabinet. You're totally *droned*! Mary Roberts shrieks. Beth scowls at her, then grabs Mary's hand and jams it against her belly, lifting her T-shirt and poking two of Mary's fingers against what looks like an appendectomy scar. Feel that? Beth says quietly, while Mary giggles. That was a present from my dad. You know what his name was, right? Big Chief Saggenballs.

Ow, says Mary, wriggling out of Beth's grasp. God, you're so *intense*.

The first time Beth and I take mushrooms, we lie on her bedroom floor and stare at the ceiling-spackle for as long as our scorched eyes can stand it. My face feels hot and huge; my cheeks are two knobs of burning fat. The air has resolved itself into a wall of churning, interlocked pinwheels, which for some reason appear only in crimson and ecru, our school's team colours. I want to tell Beth about this, but my throat has telescoped out about ten feet from my body and it's so hard to get the words through to my mouth. Besides, she is thumbing through a copy of *Maclean's* and laughing quietly to herself, and I don't want to disturb her.

Later we go to the diner near Beth's house and play the Freddy Krueger pinball game, pummelling the flipper buttons before the ball gets anywhere near them and laughing shrilly when it tumbles into the game-over slot. Good *fright*, sleep *tight*, don't let the bedbugs *bite*, Freddy says, his voice coming out in a series of digital squirts. I am *so high*, whispers Beth.

Walking home we try not to step on each other's shadows. Mine looks absurdly tall and wobbly, like old cartoons of trees in the desert or hula-dancing giraffes. I'm a giraffe, I say, feeling my chest collapse with despair at how completely lame this sounds even as I am saying it. Instead of dissolving the ego, as they are supposed to do, the mushrooms have turned me into a feedback loop of agonizing self-consciousness. I feel like a failure, even as a stoner.

When we get back to the house, Beth's mother is in the kitchen listening to a Pete Seeger tape. Did you have a nice night, girls? she asks. She looks so young, with a long grey-blonde braid and a paisley scarf around her neck, and for a second I want to ask her how often she thinks about Keanu

Reeves. My head feels emptied out and tender, and there is Beth, disappearing up the staircase without even a look in my direction. I whisper goodnight to her mother and stumble over the carpeted stairs. We fall asleep on our backs, but somehow in the night we turn like magnets, and when I wake up early in the morning I am spooning her, my hand against her ribs, and I can feel her heart beating as surely as if I were holding it, bald and leaping, in my palm.

The polar bear at the museum lives in a glass display case in the entrance hallway, frozen in a state of boredom following a seal-kill. The stuffed seal, twice dead, lies some metres away, and the bear stares into the middle distance, apparently uninterested in its quarry. Behind the bear's shoulder the fibre-optic sky goes from light blue to royal blue to black and back to light blue again in quick succession. Sometimes in the artificial night sky the aurora borealis appears, a green ghost dragging across the wall. In this hallway the sound of the north wind is always blowing.

# SALEEMA NAWAZ

## MY THREE GIRLS

There is a photo of me and Kathleen in the rec room with Maggie, our dead baby sister. She is slumped in a car seat, swaddled in a pink flannel blanket, eyes and mouth sutured shut, every crease downturned with the heaviness of death. Kathleen and I are posed to either side, legs outstretched, hips pressed into the orange carpet. We have our chins in our hands, and Kathleen has one bare foot kicked up in the air, near a couple of half-dressed Barbie dolls visible off in the corner. A picnic pose, like the one of us in Stanley Park, the checkered print of our two matching sundresses against the striped grey blanket that was our island in the sea of green grass.

We look just as relaxed in the rec room photo, our faces bright, our smiles wide and eager. Kathleen is grinning, her eyes conspiring with the camera as though she could bewitch it with a direct gaze. The sly but charming look that I can trace through all the family photos, from her class pictures to her wedding scrapbook. Beautiful Kathleen, impish at seven in our finished basement. But her smile, so beguiling and intense, barely eclipses my own, for in the photo I actually seem to be giggling, betraying my crooked teeth as my brown ponytail flails forward over my shoulder, a messy signal of movement, of the quivering motions of laughter. I can barely pick out the rims of the glasses that I used to hate, and at eleven, I seem at home in my body, unself-conscious of the exposed roll of stomach bulging out in a pale band under my purple T-shirt. The girth of my hips already large enough, as I lie lengthwise, to dwarf the car seat placed before us.

It is likely that it was our mother who told us to smile. In her album, this photo is captioned "My Three Girls."

When my husband doesn't want us to get a midwife, he cites Maggie as a reason for going to the hospital. He thinks he is at his most persuasive after dinner, when I am full and tired and tend to agree with anything.

"What about your baby sister that died? Didn't your mother have her at home?"

The cautious vagueness in his question irks me, although I know it is only his attempt at tact, at not venturing to express more than I would presume him to feel. He knows as well as anyone in the family, as well as almost anyone who ever met her, that my mother had a baby that died.

"Maggie didn't die because she was born at home," I say. "She died because she had a birth defect that would have killed her no matter where she was born."

I remember my father, dry-eyed and harried, explaining how what had happened to Maggie was not quite as sad as if she could have lived but had died anyway.

"It is a tragedy, yes," he said, and the side of his mouth sagged open in a mirror of Kathleen's openly gawking face. "A tragedy has befallen this family. But it is something closer to a disappointment than a devastation."

His exhalation at the end of this sentence, when it came, was as loud and breathy in its way as the ragged gulps and wheezes of my mother that, after the funeral, we could regularly hear coming from behind the bedroom door.

"Oh." Eric turns away for a moment, stooping under the sink for dish soap, before attempting, "But what does your mother think?"

Which is his way of saying my mother won't like it and by even considering it we're signing ourselves up for weeks of her heart-rending pleadings – speeches that will make me mourn not only my sister and the woman my mother used to be, but the way I used to be able to feel grief and pity and know that they were in no way mixed with apathy or contempt.

Until Kathleen was born, I never liked dolls. Their puckered lips and grappling fingers were nothing to me compared to the soft snout of a teddy bear or stuffed cat. Kathleen, when she came, was squishy like a plush animal and warm besides. I was captivated by her multitude of tiny expressions, sometimes even poking her in the side with my index finger to see a ripple of unhappiness clench her amazing, volatile face. I wondered how we had ever lived without her, without someone who could take us away from ourselves and the petty tedium of whatever had consumed us before.

When they brought Maggie home for the wake, she

reminded me of those old dolls, as light as though she were filled only with air, instead of with miniature organs and her still, imperfect heart. She was hard, too, like the dolls, except for her feet, which were soft and movable. My mother told us it was because the veins there were too tiny to be embalmed, and Kathleen stroked the soles of them with one finger, crooning "Cootchie-cootchie-coo" until my mother slapped her hand away and took Maggie upstairs to be passed around among the guests.

Eric is incredulous that my mother still hasn't seen the baby in anything besides the dozens of snapshots taken by Kathleen.

"Your daughter has a baby, you go," he says. I smile at him because I find his indignation, when it is on my behalf, charming. His bottom lip juts outward as his head begins a concise quiver of disapproval, his hands rubbing up and down against his striped shirt at the small of his back, in a flap-wing posture of concern. My hand on his cheek stops him, and he leans into my touch before shrugging his shoulders. He collapses into the chair beside Hannah's crib that gives the best vantage point for parental doting and gloating.

"My mother has been practically living here for the past four weeks," he says.

"I know." Laundered little outfits are folded neatly in piles near the changing table, and prepared meals are stacked deep into the freezer, their mottled surfaces speckled with frost like snow-capped peaks through the blue lids of the plastic containers. "She's been a big help."

"Well, then. Doesn't your mother care at all?"

And because there is no answer to this question that he will understand, I tell him that I will call her and invite myself over.

My mother paces the kitchen, drying dishes, stirring the soup, following a nervous course around the perimeter of the table where I am sitting with the baby. Hannah fusses in a way that is unusual for her, her mouth falling open in an expression of wild anguish, her fists balling at the ends of arms raised and quivering like a mad conductor in full orchestral swing. As I soothe her, I imagine she senses my mother's nervous energy, her inability to comprehend good news. My parents' circle narrowed with Maggie's death, whittled down to relatives and those with a taste or tolerance for grief. Even now, with the evidence of a healthy baby right before her, my mother's interest is on Hannah's narrow escape.

"So are you in a lot of pain?" she asks. My mother nods with sympathy toward my belly, which below my shirt is now scarred in a red and glistening line from the surgery that birthed my daughter.

"A little."

My mother's dire predictions of calamity have stifled certain aspects of our conversations. When, during my third trimester, I confided that I hadn't felt the baby move in a day and a half, she surmised aloud that the baby was probably dead. She still looked huffy and bewildered when Eric, arriving to pick me up, gave her only a curt hello before helping me out to the car.

My mother begins scrubbing new potatoes in the colander. She looks over at me from the sink.

"You ought to have tried to lose some of that weight before having a baby," she says. "It isn't healthy."

"That's true." I raise my eyebrows at her before looking down to stroke the side of Hannah's cheek, watching as her cries quiet down with exhaustion. "Remind me to give you your clothes back as soon as I start to drop some of these pounds."

"Oh, you." My mother shakes her head and brings the washed potatoes and a peeler to the counter nearest to the table. "It's true, you know. You shouldn't be like me."

Like a reluctant Lazarus, my mother is drawing closer to Hannah bit by bit. She grabs a handful of potato peels and steps toward the garbage can to the right of the table. On her way, I see her shoot a glance at the baby, her pupils dilating until her brown eyes are suffused in black.

"Why don't you sit down?" I kick with my foot at the chair opposite me until it budges out from the table with a clatter against the linoleum that makes Hannah open her eyes and give a small, plaintive cry.

My mother throws the peels in the garbage and settles down on the proffered chair, clucking her disapproval.

"Honestly, you should know better," she says. "Give her here. I'll quiet her."

And so I hand her the baby, and she takes her from me with strong, sure hands, her lips trembling with the start of a lullaby.

In bed at night, we pretended Maggie was a ghost who was watching us. Not an angel, because it seemed unbelievable to us, since we had seen her in her final grim repose, that she could wish us well.

"If you don't get up and close that closet door," I said, "Maggie will try and choke you to death in your sleep."

"Why would she try and do that?" Kathleen's voice was piteous in the darkness with a rehearsed tremulousness of fear. The conversation was a kind of game that we always played.

"Because she's jealous of us. Because we're alive and she isn't. Because she knows we're happy that she's gone."

"I'm not," said Kathleen.

"Yes, you are. You're happy because if she were alive you wouldn't be able to take ballet lessons because we wouldn't have enough money." I didn't know if this was true, but it struck me as a brilliant inspiration.

"Really?" There was a rustling in the darkness as Kathleen half sat up in her bed.

"Really. And she knows that you think she's ugly. She knows you told me that you thought she looked weird." Another inspiration, on my roll of cruelty. Kathleen had confided to me, in the confused weeks after the funeral, as our mother disappeared into a pile of grief-counselling books, that she thought that Maggie didn't look like a normal baby.

"She was a funny colour," she whispered to me, as our mother arranged a tiny, framed photo of Maggie on the centre of the mantelpiece, behind a white tea light. Maggie's mottled face was patchy blue and red from the poor breathing that never even really got started.

"How does Maggie know that?" asked Kathleen, who by now was fully sitting up. I could see the shadow that her rumpled hair cast against the wall by the glow of our snowflake night-light. "Will she tell Mummy?"

"No," I said, and my shoulders shook in a sudden quake as

I pictured a bundled Maggie hovering near my mother's sleeping face. Sometimes I even scared myself in these late-night chats. "No, I don't think so."

In the waiting room, Kathleen looks healthier than the other patients, her hair cut short but grown thicker than ever, and I can see them turning to me, peeking up from the aged magazines to scout my body for the signs of sickness, for a benchmark of suffering against which they can measure their own recovery or decline. I can see the conclusions forming, a speculation of tumours hidden under layers of fat, the defensive attributions of blame upon an obese woman for a disease she must have brought upon herself. Next to my sister, I look like the one who deserves to be struck down.

But if they look up from Kathleen's stomach, and its promising bulge upon which she has folded her pale, dry hands, they might notice the boyish plane of her chest and a fierce clenching of the jaw that has drawn down her winning smile into the wryest grin imaginable – the only visible traces of her illness since remission. Back then she claimed that she wouldn't miss her breasts, calling them her "bad luck magnets."

"What did they ever do for me?" she said, sipping water from a hospital paper cup as though it might be a daiquiri, or the sangria we used to mix in a bucket when we went to the lake in the summer. "Besides getting me a couple of bad boyfriends and a loser of an ex-husband?" She giggled. Greg was an angel, a formalist poet she divorced when she began sleeping with his brother. After the affair and a couple of aggrieved sonnets, Greg was now her most devoted friend.

"Not to mention cancer."

"Exactly."

My cheeks ached from our nervy, hysterical laughter behind the curtain of the pink recovery room, and I didn't look away because the only thing back then, the only thing that could make Kathleen upset, was for someone to look away from her, to drop their gaze from the sight of her skinny, determined face.

There are other photos of Maggie. A whole album of them sat on the mantelpiece for a year after her death, until my father removed it to an upstairs closet. It is a small, square album, bound in white leather, with only one photograph per page. Documenting my youngest sister from her conception to her funeral, its first few pages consist of side-profile shots of my mother's pregnant belly, the smooth roundness covered in a bright floral print that almost matches the wallpaper, her stomach like a balloon emerging in high relief. The next six pages hold a series of photographs showing Maggie's brief stay in the plastic bassinette of the ICU, tubes obscuring her face and small body. Beneath the fifth photograph taken at the hospital, my mother has written, in her neat and regular handwriting, "This is the last photo of Maggie alive."

Most of the rest of the photos are snapshots taken at the wake, with various friends and relatives holding Maggie's embalmed body, their tight and solemn faces barely concealing their horror. The very last photograph in the book is of my parents huddled on the gravesite before the funeral. The tiny white coffin sits ready for burial on the grass before them, projecting a sturdy kind of cheerfulness as it gleams in the sunlight, while my mother, slumped against my father, looks like a pantomime of woe. He sits cross-legged, face downcast, his arm around her shoulders, and yet I project upon him an invisible embarrassment, an awareness of the professional photographer who must have staged the tableau of grief.

My father is dead now, too, but there are no photographs of his grave or of the small ceremony attended not only by our family but by his students from the university. He suffered a stroke on his way home from a lecture and died, the next day, without opening his eyes. When I called Kathleen to tell her to come to the hospital, she was already there for radiation treatment. Our mother, who was bracing herself for a different disaster, whispered to me as we pulled up in the cab, "He doesn't want to live to see another child die."

"He didn't do this on purpose," I said, but she was already hurrying inside, the sound of her wheezes and her heavy, uneven footsteps still audible from the pavement.

It's obvious that the doctor is angry at Kathleen. She is clutching her clipboard to her chest, her eyes glancing over at me instead of my sister. It is the irritability and embarrassment of bad news. The doctor is normally very pleasant.

"We knew that this could happen," she says. "We knew it was a risk."

"I know," says Kathleen.

"This is why we tell people to wait at least two years."

"I know," repeats Kathleen. "I'm not blaming you." She shrugs, and in an oncology office the gesture has a fatalistic bravado that makes my heart sink. "It could have come back anyways, even if I didn't stop taking the drugs."

The doctor is shaking her head, her face severe as she talks about lymph nodes and advanced stages, and Kathleen is nodding. I wonder why I didn't try and talk my sister out of it eight months ago, when she told me that she was undergoing tests to find out if her eggs were still viable since her treatment.

"When do you get the results back?" I'd asked. I tried to curb the grin I could feel spreading over my face, for I had begun to feel superstitious since Kathleen's illness and our father's death. As though Maggie, lonesome and implacable, was still watching us for signs of too much happiness.

Kathleen laughed as she bounced Hannah on her knee. "I don't know exactly. It's a kind of self-administered test." She winked at me. "Greg's helping."

Now Kathleen is saying, "I don't want to hurt the baby. After she's born I'll do whatever you think is best." She struggles out of the chair with the help of my hand and adds, "If it's worth it."

Sometimes when Hannah is quiet and I am holding her against my body, or she is strapped into the sling carrier, dozing, I imagine that I am still pregnant, that the cancer that killed my sister is still being held at bay, and that Kathleen is not another tragedy to be added to my mother's litany of sorrow. My breathing slows, and my eyes begin closing until she stirs and I let reality surge back, traces of guilt lapping at the edge of consciousness. But I don't wish Hannah away, only back inside, buffeted from my helplessness at keeping people safe.

Setting Hannah down on the playmat, I bring Meghan to my breast to be fed, as I did even before her mother passed away. She looks enough like Hannah to be her sister, though her features are always changing, her face first looking longer, then rounder. Her blue eyes looking darker, then wiser.

My mother is moving around in the next room, asking aloud how I ever let my bathtub get so filthy, until she drowns herself out by turning on the taps. She stays over during the week now, helping with the house and the babies. But sometimes I catch her looking at me as though she can't understand why she was left with the least promising one, the heavy one that takes life too seriously, the one the most like her. And at night, when I get up to check on the babies, each sleeping in a crib in the nursery, I sometimes see my mother walking from room to room, her face sagging in grief, looking like a lost little girl.

**Théodora Armstrong** is a fiction writer and poet who lives in Vancouver, British Columbia. Her work has appeared in numerous literary magazines such as *Event*, *Prairie Fire*, *Grain Magazine*, *The Fiddlehead*, *Descant*, *The New Quarterly*, and *Contemporary Verse 2*, and has also been nominated for a National Magazine Award. "Whale Stories" won the Western Magazine Award for Fiction. She holds an M.F.A. in Creative Writing from the University of British Columbia, where she recently completed a collection of short fiction. She is now at work on her first novel.

**Mike Christie** was born in Thunder Bay and now lives in Vancouver, where he's finishing his M.F.A. in Creative Writing at the University of British Columbia. He's worked in homeless shelters and psychiatric care facilities, and at this very moment he's working on a collection of short fiction. *Goodbye Porkpie Hat* is his first published story.

**Anna Leventhal** is a writer and performing artist living in Montreal. Her writing has appeared as feature fiction in *Geist*, and she placed second in the 2005 *Annual Geist Literal Literary Postcard Story Competition*. She has presented theatrical work at performance art festivals across North America, and her experimental documentary *Ten Thousand Faces I've Never Seen* was broadcast on CBC Radio One. She is the contributing editor of *The Art of Trespassing*, an anthology of short fiction put out by Invisible Publishing.

**Naomi K. Lewis** has published stories and poetry in Canadian journals including *Grain*, *The New Quarterly*, *The Antigonish Review*, and *Prairie Fire*. Her story "The Guiding Light," cut from an early draft of her novel, *Cricket in a Fist* (Goose Lane Editions, 2008), won the 2007 Fiddlehead Fiction Prize and will appear in *No Such Thing as a Free Ride?*, an anthology of stories about hitchhiking. Naomi has a habit of moving every few years, and currently lives in Edmonton.

**Oscar Martens** has published twenty-one pieces in literary journals across Canada. His short story collection, *The Girl With the Full Figure Is Your Daughter*, was published by Turnstone Press in 2002. He has recently completed another collection. Although currently living in Coquitlam, Oscar has lived in Victoria, Winnipeg, Ottawa, Kenya, and New Zealand.

**Dana Mills**'s fiction has appeared in *Geist*. Born and raised in idyllic rural Nova Scotia, he lives and works in a cubicle in Toronto. He is completing a collection of stories entitled *Blueprints for an Early Death*.

**Saleema Nawaz**'s short fiction has appeared in literary journals such as *Prairie Fire*, *PRISM international*, *Grain*, and *The New Quarterly*. Freehand Books is publishing her first collection, *Mother Superior*, in Fall 2008. Born in Ottawa, she attended Carleton University and completed an M.A. in English Literature at the University of Manitoba in 2006. She now lives in Montreal, where she is at work on a novel.

**Scott Randall** is the author of two short story collections published by Signature Editions, *Last Chance to Renew* (2006) and, most recently, *Character Actor* (2008), which includes "The Gifted Class." His fiction has appeared in *The Antigonish Review*, *The Dalhousie Review*, *Event*, *The Malahat Review*, *The New Quarterly*, and *The Journey Prize Stories 18*.

**S. Kennedy Sobol** grew up in Eastern Ontario, and now lives in Toronto. "Some Light Down" appeared in *PRISM international* and is her first published story. She is currently at work on a short story collection.

**Sarah Steinberg** writes short stories, book reviews, and funny li'l things. She is currently working on a handful of projects, including a children's book called *Tommy Age Six and the Big Huge Dump*. Her first collection of short stories will be published by Insomniac Press in the summer of 2008.

**Clea Young**'s poetry and short fiction have appeared in numerous Canadian literary magazines, and one of her stories has been anthologized in an earlier volume of *The Journey Prize Stories*. She holds a Masters of Fine Arts in Creative Writing from the University of British Columbia and currently lives in Vancouver, where she is working on a collection of stories and a novella.

For more information about all the journals that submitted stories to this year's anthology, please consult *The Journey Prize Stories* website: www.mcclelland.com/jps.

**The Dalhousie Review** has been in operation since 1921 and aspires to be a forum in which seriousness of purpose and playfulness of mind can coexist in meaningful dialogue. The journal publishes new fiction and poetry in every issue and welcomes submissions from authors around the world. Editor: Anthony Stewart. Submissions and correspondence: *The Dalhousie Review*, Dalhousie University, Halifax, Nova Scotia, B3H 4R2. Email: dalhousie.review@dal.ca Website: www.dalhousiereview.dal.ca

Now in its thirty-seventh year of publication, **Event** is a celebrated literary journal in which readers can encounter new and established talent – in fiction, poetry, non-fiction, and critical reviews. The journal thrives on a balance of both traditional narrative and contemporary approaches to poetry and prose. *Event* is home to Canada's longest-running annual non-fiction contest. It is our goal to support and encourage a thriving literary community in Canada, while maintaining our international reputation for excellence. Editor: Rick Maddocks. Managing Editor: Ian Cockfield. Fiction Editor: Christine Dewar. Poetry Editor: Elizabeth Bachinsky. Submissions and correspondence:

*Event*, P.O. Box 2503, New Westminster, British Columbia, V3L 5B2. Email (queries only): event@douglas.bc.ca Website: www.event.douglas.bc.ca

**The Fiddlehead**, Atlantic Canada's longest-running literary journal, publishes poetry and short fiction as well as book reviews. It appears four times a year and sponsors a contest for poetry and fiction that awards a total of $4,000 in prizes, including the $1,000 Ralph Gustafson Poetry Prize. *The Fiddlehead* welcomes all good writing in English, from anywhere, looking always for that element of freshness and surprise. Editor: Ross Leckie. Managing Editor: Kathryn Taglia. Submissions and correspondence: *The Fiddlehead*, Campus House, 11 Garland Court, University of New Brunswick, P.O. Box 4400, Fredericton, New Brunswick, E3B 5A3. Email (queries only): fiddlehd@unb.ca Website: www.lib.unb.ca/Texts/Fiddlehead

**Geist** is a Canadian magazine of ideas and culture, with a strong literary focus, a special interest in photography, and a sense of humour. The *Geist* tone is intelligent, plain-talking, inclusive, and offbeat. Each issue is a strangely convergent collection of fiction, non-fiction, photographs, comix, reviews, little-known facts of interest, a bit of poetry, and the legendary *Geist* map and crossword puzzle, all of which explore the lines between fiction and non-fiction, and take a new look at Canada, the country we are all still in the process of imagining. Editor: Stephen Osborne. Submissions and correspondence: *Geist*, #200 – 341 Water Street, Vancouver, British Columbia, V6B 1B8. Email: geist@geist.com Website: www.geist.com

**Grain Magazine** provides readers with fine, fresh writing by new and established writers of poetry and prose four times a year. Published by the Saskatchewan Writers Guild, *Grain* has earned national and international recognition for its distinctive literary content. Editor: Kent Bruyneel. Fiction Editor: Dave Margoshes. Poetry Editor: Gerald Hill. Submissions and correspondence: *Grain Magazine*, P.O. Box 67, Saskatoon, Saskatchewan, S7K 3K1. Email: grainmag@sasktel.net Website: www.grainmagazine.ca

**Prairie Fire** is a quarterly magazine of contemporary Canadian writing that publishes stories, poems, and literary non-fiction by both emerging and established writers. *Prairie Fire*'s editorial mix also occasionally features critical or personal essays and interviews with authors. Stories published in *Prairie Fire* have won awards at the National Magazine Awards and the Western Magazine Awards. *Prairie Fire* publishes writing from, and has readers in, all parts of Canada. Editor: Andris Taskans. Fiction Editors: Warren Cariou and Heidi Harms. Submissions and correspondence: *Prairie Fire*, Room 423–100 Arthur Street, Winnipeg, Manitoba, R3B 1H3. Email: prfire@mts.net Website: www.prairiefire.ca

**PRISM international**, the oldest literary magazine in Western Canada, was established in 1959 by a group of Vancouver writers. Published four times a year, *PRISM* features short fiction, poetry, drama, creative non-fiction, and translations by both new and established writers from Canada and around the world. The only criteria are originality and quality. *PRISM* holds three exemplary competitions: the Short

Fiction Contest, the Literary Non-fiction Contest, and the Earle Birney Prize for Poetry. Executive Editors: Krista Eide and Kristjanna Grimmelt. Fiction Editor: Michelle Miller. Poetry Editor: Crystal Sikma. Submissions and correspondence: *PRISM international*, Creative Writing Program, The University of British Columbia, Buchanan E-462, 1866 Main Mall, Vancouver, British Columbia, V6T 1Z1. Email (for queries only): prism@interchange.ubc.ca Website: www.prismmagazine.ca

**Queen's Quarterly**, founded in 1893, is the oldest intellectual journal in Canada. It publishes articles on a variety of subjects and, consequently, fiction occupies relatively little space. There are one or two stories in each issue. However, because of its lively format and eclectic mix of subject matter, *Queen's Quarterly* attracts readers with widely diverse interests. This exposure is an advantage many of our fiction writers appreciate. Submissions are welcome from both new and established writers. Literary Editor: Joan Harcourt. Submissions and correspondence: *Queen's Quarterly*, Queen's University, 144 Barrie Street, Kingston, Ontario, K7L 3N6. Email: queens.quarterly@queensu.ca Website: www.queensu.ca/quarterly

**subTerrain Magazine**, which turns twenty years strong in 2008, publishes contemporary and sometimes controversial Canadian fiction, poetry, non-fiction, and visual art. Every issue features interviews, timely commentary, and book reviews. Praised by both writers and readers for featuring work that might not find a home in more conservative periodicals, *subTerrain Magazine* seeks to expand the definition of Canadian literary and artistic culture by showcasing the best in progressive writing and ideas. Please visit our website for more information on upcoming theme issues, our annual Lush Triumphant contest, general submission guidelines, and subscription information. Submissions and correspondence: *subTerrain Magazine*, P.O. Box 3008, MPO, Vancouver, British Columbia, V6B 3X5. Website: www.subterrain.ca

For more than four decades, **This Magazine** has proudly published fiction and poetry from new and emerging Canadian writers. A sassy and thoughtful journal of arts, politics, and pop culture, *This* consistently offers fresh takes on familiar issues, as well as breaking stories that need to be told. Publisher: Lisa Whittington-Hill. Fiction & Poetry Editor: Stuart Ross. Correspondence: *This Magazine*, Suite 396 – 401 Richmond Ave. W., Toronto, Ontario, M5V 3A8. Website: www.thismagazine.ca

Submissions were also received from the following journals:

*The Antigonish Review*
(Antigonish, N.S.)

*Matrix Magazine*
(Montreal, Que.)

*Broken Pencil*
(Toronto, Ont.)

*The New Orphic Review*
(Nelson, B.C.)

*The Capilano Review*
(North Vancouver, B.C.)

*The New Quarterly*
(Waterloo, Ont.)

*The Claremont Review*
(Victoria, B.C.)

*On Spec*
(Edmonton, Alta.)

*dANDelion*
(Calgary, Alta.)

*Prairie Journal*
(Calgary, Alta.)

*Descant*
(Toronto, Ont.)

*Room Magazine*
(Vancouver, B.C.)

*Exile: The Literary Quarterly*
(Toronto, Ont.)

*Storyteller*
(Ottawa, Ont.)

*Maisonneuve Magazine*
(Montreal, Que.)

*Taddle Creek*
(Toronto, Ont.)

*The Malahat Review*
(Victoria, B.C.)

*Vancouver Review*
(Vancouver, B.C.)

# PREVIOUS CONTRIBUTING AUTHORS

* Winners of the $10,000 Journey Prize
** Co-winners of the $10,000 Journey Prize

I

1989

### SELECTED WITH ALISTAIR MacLEOD

Ven Begamudré, "Word Games"

David Bergen, "Where You're From"

Lois Braun, "The Pumpkin-Eaters"

Constance Buchanan, "Man with Flying Genitals"

Ann Copeland, "Obedience"

Marion Douglas, "Flags"

Frances Itani, "An Evening in the Café"

Diane Keating, "The Crying Out"

Thomas King, "One Good Story, That One"

Holley Rubinsky, "Rapid Transits"*

Jean Rysstad, "Winter Baby"

Kevin Van Tighem, "Whoopers"

M.G. Vassanji, "In the Quiet of a Sunday Afternoon"

Bronwen Wallace, "Chicken 'N' Ribs"

Armin Wiebe, "Mouse Lake"

Budge Wilson, "Waiting"

2

1990

### SELECTED WITH LEON ROOKE; GUY VANDERHAEGHE

André Alexis, "Despair: Five Stories of Ottawa"

Glen Allen, "The Hua Guofeng Memorial Warehouse"

Marusia Bociurkiw, "Mama, Donya"

Virgil Burnett, "Billfrith the Dreamer"

Margaret Dyment, "Sacred Trust"

Cynthia Flood, "My Father Took a Cake to France"*

Douglas Glover, "Story Carved in Stone"

Terry Griggs, "Man with the Axe"

Rick Hillis, "Limbo River"

Thomas King, "The Dog I Wish I Had, I Would Call It Helen"

K.D. Miller, "Sunrise Till Dark"

Jennifer Mitton, "Let Them Say"

Lawrence O'Toole, "Goin' to Town with Katie Ann"

Kenneth Radu, "A Change of Heart"

Jenifer Sutherland, "Table Talk"

Wayne Tefs, "Red Rock and After"

3

1991

### SELECTED WITH JANE URQUHART

Donald Aker, "The Invitation"

Anton Baer, "Yukon"

Allan Barr, "A Visit from Lloyd"

David Bergen, "The Fall"

Rai Berzins, "Common Sense"

Diana Hartog, "Theories of Grief"

Diane Keating, "The Salem Letters"

Yann Martel, "The Facts Behind the Helsinki Roccamatios"*

Jennifer Mitton, "Polaroid"

Sheldon Oberman, "This Business with Elijah"

Lynn Podgurny, "Till Tomorrow, Maple Leaf Mills"

James Riseborough, "She Is Not His Mother" ·

Patricia Stone, "Living on the Lake"


4

1992

### SELECTED WITH SANDRA BIRDSELL

David Bergen, "The Bottom of the Glass"

Maria A. Billion, "No Miracles Sweet Jesus"

Judith Cowan, "By the Big River"

Steven Heighton, "A Man Away from Home Has No Neighbours"

Steven Heighton, "How Beautiful upon the Mountains"

L. Rex Kay, "Travelling"

Rozena Maart, "No Rosa, No District Six"*

Guy Malet De Carteret, "Rainy Day"

Carmelita McGrath, "Silence"

Michael Mirolla, "A Theory of Discontinuous Existence"

Diane Juttner Perreault, "Bella's Story"

Eden Robinson, "Traplines"


5

1993

### SELECTED WITH GUY VANDERHAEGHE

Caroline Adderson, "Oil and Dread"

David Bergen, "La Rue Prevette"

Marina Endicott, "With the Band"

Dayv James-French, "Cervine"

Michael Kenyon, "Durable Tumblers"

K.D. Miller, "A Litany in Time of Plague"

Robert Mullen, "Flotsam"

Gayla Reid, "Sister Doyle's Men"*

Oakland Ross, "Bang-bang"

Robert Sherrin, "Technical Battle for Trial Machine"

Carol Windley, "The Etruscans"

## 6

### 1994

#### SELECTED WITH DOUGLAS GLOVER;

#### JUDITH CHANT (CHAPTERS)

Anne Carson, "Water Margins: An Essay on Swimming by My
    Brother"

Richard Cumyn, "The Sound He Made"

Genni Gunn, "Versions"

Melissa Hardy, "Long Man the River"*

Robert Mullen, "Anomie"

Vivian Payne, "Free Falls"

Jim Reil, "Dry"

Robyn Sarah, "Accept My Story"

Joan Skogan, "Landfall"

Dorothy Speak, "Relatives in Florida"

Alison Wearing, "Notes from Under Water"

7

1995

SELECTED WITH M.G. VASSANJI;

RICHARD BACHMANN (A DIFFERENT DRUMMER BOOKS)

Michelle Alfano, "Opera"

Mary Borsky, "Maps of the Known World"

Gabriella Goliger, "Song of Ascent"

Elizabeth Hay, "Hand Games"

Shaena Lambert, "The Falling Woman"

Elise Levine, "Boy"

Roger Burford Mason, "The Rat-Catcher's Kiss"

Antanas Sileika, "Going Native"

Kathryn Woodward, "Of Marranos and Gilded Angels"*

8

1996

SELECTED WITH OLIVE SENIOR;

BEN MCNALLY (NICHOLAS HOARE LTD.)

Rick Bowers, "Dental Bytes"

David Elias, "How I Crossed Over"

Elyse Gasco, "Can You Wave Bye Bye, Baby?"*

Danuta Gleed, "Bones"

Elizabeth Hay, "The Friend"

Linda Holeman, "Turning the Worm"

Elaine Littman, "The Winner's Circle"

Murray Logan, "Steam"

Rick Maddocks, "Lessons from the Sputnik Diner"

K.D. Miller, "Egypt Land"

Gregor Robinson, "Monster Gaps"

Alma Subasic, "Dust"

9

1997

SELECTED WITH NINO RICCI; NICHOLAS PASHLEY

(UNIVERSITY OF TORONTO BOOKSTORE)

Brian Bartlett, "Thomas, Naked"

Dennis Bock, "Olympia"

Kristen den Hartog, "Wave"

Gabriella Goliger, "Maladies of the Inner Ear"**

Terry Griggs, "Momma Had a Baby"

Mark Anthony Jarman, "Righteous Speedboat"

Judith Kalman, "Not for Me a Crown of Thorns"

Andrew Mullins, "The World of Science"

Sasenarine Persaud, "Canada Geese and Apple Chatney"

Anne Simpson, "Dreaming Snow"**

Sarah Withrow, "Ollie"

Terence Young, "The Berlin Wall"


10

1998

SELECTED BY PETER BUITENHUIS; HOLLEY RUBINSKY;

CELIA DUTHIE (DUTHIE BOOKS LTD.)

John Brooke, "The Finer Points of Apples"*

Ian Colford, "The Reason for the Dream"

Libby Creelman, "Cruelty"

Michael Crummey, "Serendipity"

Stephen Guppy, "Downwind"

Jane Eaton Hamilton, "Graduation"

Elise Levine, "You Are You Because Your Little Dog Loves You"

Jean McNeil, "Bethlehem"

Liz Moore, "Eight-Day Clock"

Edward O'Connor, "The Beatrice of Victoria College"

Tim Rogers, "Scars and Other Presents"

Denise Ryan, "Marginals, Vivisections, and Dreams"

Madeleine Thien, "Simple Recipes"

Cheryl Tibbetts, "Flowers of Africville"


II

1999

SELECTED BY LESLEY CHOYCE; SHELDON CURRIE;

MARY-JO ANDERSON (FROG HOLLOW BOOKS)

Mike Barnes, "In Florida"

Libby Creelman, "Sunken Island"

Mike Finigan, "Passion Sunday"

Jane Eaton Hamilton, "Territory"

Mark Anthony Jarman, "Travels into Several Remote Nations of the
    World"

Barbara Lambert, "Where the Bodies Are Kept"

Linda Little, "The Still"

Larry Lynch, "The Sitter"

Sandra Sabatini, "The One With the News"

Sharon Steams, "Brothers"

Mary Walters, "Show Jumping"

Alissa York, "The Back of the Bear's Mouth"*

12

2000

SELECTED BY CATHERINE BUSH; HAL NIEDZVIECKI;

MARC GLASSMAN (PAGES BOOKS AND MAGAZINES)

Andrew Gray, "The Heart of the Land"

Lee Henderson, "Sheep Dub"

Jessica Johnson, "We Move Slowly"

John Lavery, "The Premier's New Pyjamas"

J.A. McCormack, "Hearsay"

Nancy Richler, "Your Mouth Is Lovely"

Andrew Smith, "Sightseeing"

Karen Solie, "Onion Calendar"

Timothy Taylor, "Doves of Townsend"*

Timothy Taylor, "Pope's Own"

Timothy Taylor, "Silent Cruise"

R.M. Vaughan, "Swan Street"

13

2001

SELECTED BY ELYSE GASCO; MICHAEL HELM;

MICHAEL NICHOLSON (INDIGO BOOKS & MUSIC INC.)

Kevin Armstrong, "The Cane Field"*

Mike Barnes, "Karaoke Mon Amour"

Heather Birrell, "Machaya"

Heather Birrell, "The Present Perfect"

Craig Boyko, "The Gun"

Vivette J. Kady, "Anything That Wiggles"

Billie Livingston, "You're Taking All the Fun Out of It"

Annabel Lyon, "Fishes"

Lisa Moore, "The Way the Light Is"

Heather O'Neill, "Little Suitcase"

Susan Rendell, "In the Chambers of the Sea"

Tim Rogers, "Watch"

Margrith Schraner, "Dream Dig"

## 14

### 2002

#### SELECTED BY ANDRÉ ALEXIS;

#### DEREK MCCORMACK; DIANE SCHOEMPERLEN

Mike Barnes, "Cogagwee"

Geoffrey Brown, "Listen"

Jocelyn Brown, "Miss Canada"*

Emma Donoghue, "What Remains"

Jonathan Goldstein, "You Are a Spaceman With Your Head Under the
    Bathroom Stall Door"

Robert McGill, "Confidence Men"

Robert McGill, "The Stars Are Falling"

Nick Melling, "Philemon"

Robert Mullen, "Alex the God"

Karen Munro, "The Pool"

Leah Postman, "Being Famous"

Neil Smith, "Green Fluorescent Protein"

## 15

### 2003

#### SELECTED BY MICHELLE BERRY;

#### TIMOTHY TAYLOR; MICHAEL WINTER

Rosaria Campbell, "Reaching"

Hilary Dean, "The Lemon Stories"

Dawn Rae Downton, "Hansel and Gretel"

Anne Fleming, "Gay Dwarves of America"

Elyse Friedman, "Truth"

Charlotte Gill, "Hush"

Jessica Grant, "My Husband's Jump"*

Jacqueline Honnet, "Conversion Classes"

S.K. Johannesen, "Resurrection"

Avner Mandelman, "Cuckoo"

Tim Mitchell, "Night Finds Us"

Heather O'Neill, "The Difference Between Me and Goldstein"

16

2004

SELECTED BY ELIZABETH HAY;

LISA MOORE; MICHAEL REDHILL

Anar Ali, "Baby Khaki's Wings"

Kenneth Bonert, "Packers and Movers"

Jennifer Clouter, "Benny and the Jets"

Daniel Griffin, "Mercedes Buyer's Guide"

Michael Kissinger, "Invest in the North"

Devin Krukoff, "The Last Spark"*

Elaine McCluskey, "The Watermelon Social"

William Metcalfe, "Nice Big Car, Rap Music Coming
    Out the Window"

Lesley Millard, "The Uses of the Neckerchief"

Adam Lewis Schroeder, "Burning the Cattle at Both Ends"

Michael V. Smith, "What We Wanted"

Neil Smith, "Isolettes"

Patricia Rose Young, "Up the Clyde on a Bike"

## 17
### 2005

SELECTED BY JAMES GRAINGER AND NANCY LEE

Randy Boyagoda, "Rice and Curry Yacht Club"

Krista Bridge, "A Matter of Firsts"

Josh Byer, "Rats, Homosex, Saunas, and Simon"

Craig Davidson, "Failure to Thrive"

McKinley M. Hellenes, "Brighter Thread"

Catherine Kidd, "Green-Eyed Beans"

Pasha Malla, "The Past Composed"

Edward O'Connor, "Heard Melodies Are Sweet"

Barbara Romanik, "Seven Ways into Chandigarh"

Sandra Sabatini, "The Dolphins at Sainte Marie"

Matt Shaw, "Matchbook for a Mother's Hair"*

Richard Simas, "Anthropologies"

Neil Smith, "Scrapbook"

Emily White, "Various Metals"

## 18
### 2006

SELECTED BY STEVEN GALLOWAY;

ZSUZSI GARTNER; ANNABEL LYON

Heather Birrell, "BriannaSusannaAlana"*

Craig Boyko, "The Baby"

Craig Boyko, "The Beloved Departed"

Nadia Bozak, "Heavy Metal Housekeeping"

Lee Henderson, "Conjugation"

Melanie Little, "Wrestling"

Matthew Rader, "The Lonesome Death of Joseph Fey"

Scott Randall, "Law School"

Sarah Selecky, "Throwing Cotton"

Damian Tarnopolsky, "Sleepy"

Martin West, "Cretacea"

David Whitton, "The Eclipse"

Clea Young, "Split"

## 19

### 2007

SELECTED BY CAROLINE ADDERSON;

DAVID BEZMOZGIS; DIONNE BRAND

Andrew J. Borkowski, "Twelve Versions of Lech"

Craig Boyko, "OZY"*

Grant Buday, "The Curve of the Earth"

Nicole Dixon, "High-water Mark"

Krista Foss, "Swimming in Zanzibar"

Pasha Malla, "Respite"

Alice Petersen, "After Summer"

Patricia Robertson, "My Hungarian Sister"

Rebecca Rosenblum, "Chilly Girl"

Nicholas Ruddock, "How Eunice Got Her Baby"

Jean Van Loon, "Stardust"